G. Bigg-Wither

The Three Curates

Vol. I

G. Bigg-Wither

The Three Curates
Vol. I

ISBN/EAN: 9783337044909

Printed in Europe, USA, Canada, Australia, Japan

Cover: Foto ©Andreas Hilbeck / pixelio.de

More available books at **www.hansebooks.com**

THE THREE CURATES.

THE THREE CURATES.

A Novel.

BY

Mrs. G. BIGG-WITHER,

Author of "BROKEN SUNSHINE."

" Nothing is new ; we walk where others went ;
There's no vice now but has its precedent."
—HERRICK.

IN THREE VOLUMES.

VOL. I.

LONDON

F. V. WHITE & CO.,

31, SOUTHAMPTON STREET, STRAND.

THE THREE CURATES

CHAPTER I.

TEN years ago, Langton was a fair-sized market town, many miles from the metropolis. It was irregular, as old towns generally are, and its architecture commonplace and old-fashioned.

There were only one or two fairly wide thoroughfares, and these were paved with clean, wholesome red brick. But generally the streets were narrow, so that on market days some skill was required to engineer the various vehicles, so as to avoid collisions.

There was a large, square market-place, and behind this the Market Hall, where the healthy, rosy country-women sold their butter, eggs and other produce. This place was clean, cool and draughty and much frequented.

The town possessed a mayor and town council, and all the other paraphernalia of small and important dignity.

It was a loyal town, though at times party feeling ran high, and this was especially so between Church and Dissent. The *élite* of the town and neighbourhood were " Church " of rather advanced type, and generally Tories, while the rank and file were unmistakable Dissenters and Radicals.

But there were times when the various factions fused, and this was when they were threatened with any outside interference or suggestions from metropolitan authorities or neighbouring boroughs. Then they turned with one face to meet the foe. They neither wanted innovations, improvements or advice. They were perfectly satisfied with their own easy-going, substantial, respectable commonplace.

They arranged their affairs with very little regard to outside opinion. Martinmas, Candlemas, statute fairs with an assemblage in the market-place of quack doctors, cheap-jacks, gingerbread stalls, learned pigs, fat ladies, travelling circuses, afforded them interesting landmarks of the various seasons.

There was a beautiful and stately old church, which all took pride in, as being the Town's! And the Rector, a Canon of Oswald Minster, was looked up to as a gentleman and a dignitary, and to be treated accordingly by his opponents in faith.

To this Church of St. Just were attached three curates, of whom more anon.

The houses of Langton were a source of perpetual surprise to strangers. In the

1*

narrow streets these dwellings were sheer
on to the pathway. There was hardly a
front door worth speaking of; but these
small portals were models of cleanliness.
Their bright brass knockers and door
handles flashed in the sunlight, while the
one or two small steps vied with each other
in whiteness. It was only when the doors
were opened you saw what possibilities and
capabilities the houses were equal to.
Such lovely vistas of green trees and
exquisite colours greeted the eye. Nearly
all the best rooms in the house opened,
or looked on to charming old gardens,
full of old-fashioned flowers—primroses
and lilac, roses and lilies, sweet peas climb-
ing in wanton luxury, London pride, and
all the homely old flowers of childhood,
while the mossy turf, and the shady old
trees gave a delicious sense of peace and
repose ; and then you understood why

these houses showed their severely respectable fronts to the street.

In one of these dwellings, extra neat,
extra polished, lived Mrs. Frostick—the
" Mrs. Candour " of Langton. She was a
very well known, if not entirely beloved,
person. She was of uncertain age; but
anyway, she wore a brown front, severe
and straight, without any illusion, and this
gave to her small, sharp black eyes, her
long, pointed nose and wrinkled face, an
expression of keenness which often merged
into malice. She was rather given to fine
colours in dress, and altogether was a most
inconvenient old woman. She knew everybody's age—which she was very fond of
proclaiming—likewise their public and
private affairs, and she possessed that very
unpleasant, if honest, habit of calling a
spade a spade. Few people liked her; no
one thought it advisable to offend her. She

was often, indeed, propitiated with season-
able gifts. For the rest, her husband had
long since migrated to a better world, and
had left her master of the situation—in
which he had only played a most insignificant (and, people do say, a not very
comfortable) part. Her house was a model
of exquisite cleanliness, and her old servant,
Betty, a second edition of herself—only
under authority, which her mistress was
not.

A few doors off, lived the Browns, and
of this Mrs. Frostick the Brown girls stood
in perpetual uneasiness. Whenever she
came in contact with them, she always
availed herself of the privilege of an old
friend of showing up their little weaknesses,
—and certainly there was much that was
weak in them. There was Matilda, otherwise Tilly, who posed for five-and-twenty,
and was in point of fact four-and-thirty—

tall, thin, towzley about the head, with a
faded face, pale blue eyes, large hands of
the bony type, and with no particular
vices—Harriet, the second Miss Brown, a
year or two younger, a little brighter, a
little fatter, with her hair worn down to
her eyes (which were not bad), and cut
short behind like a boy's. She went in for
the " Bébé " style generally. But each of
these young ladies were agreed in one
thing, which was their business in life—a
husband at any cost.

Old David Brown, their father, was a kind-
hearted, humble-minded old man, whose
father had been a foreman, whose grand-
father had been a labourer, and he himself
was a retired farmer, with a modest little
competence. These family details he was
never tired of airing! It was a source of
pride to him, that he could look back with
honest self-respect to the labouring grand-

father and the steadily accumulating
capital, which had centred in him, "all
got, sir, by honest toil and shrewd good
sense." But his daughters by no means
shared this family pride—to them, it was
a source of perpetual mortification. They
only desired to bury their ancestors well
out of sight. But Mrs. Frostick would
never allow this! On the contrary she
was very fond of pointing a moral with the
aid of the Messrs. Brown deceased.

Mr. Brown was, like Sancho Panza, fond
of good eating and drinking, and his taste
in this respect was always gratified, for the
virtues of his two daughters in this line
were prominent. They *were* good house-
keepers. His wife had been dead many
years.

He liked also to smoke his nightly pipe at
the " Queen's Head," and on market days
generally dined at " The Ordinary," where

he weekly met his old friends. Time marched kindly with him; he had earned his rest, and he desired nothing more in life, than to be "comfortable," and that he most certainly was.

The Miss Browns were ever struggling to get into the clique just above themselves, and cliques in country towns are a very expressive if unwritten code. Of course these young ladies figured largely at tea meetings, bazaars, sunday school treats, &c., offered unlimited incense to the younger clergy, for generally speaking, there is not much other amusement provided in country towns, but that well leavened with the clerical element. And as long as curates lasted, there was always hope for Tilly and Harriet Brown.

CHAPTER II.

THE beautiful old church was snugly situated in the heart of the town. Its bells were sending forth the hour of six! Evensong was just over. The small congregation, mostly feminine, were filing out, and two of the curates, who were waiting to see the last petticoat lingeringly disappear, came out of the vestry.

"I wonder why Lanyon didn't turn up this afternoon? I quite expected him," said Percy Blythe the senior. "He is out of quarantine now. I hope, though, he *isn't* in for small-pox! it would be small wonder, considering how he has been associating day after day with those wretched gipsies. He said he felt seedy this morning."

"It's just as likely he has had another

influx of slippers, or letters. That's enough to put him out of gear for the rest of the day," replied Mr. Dashwood with a cold smile.

"I say Cyril! suppose we go and hunt him up, we can let the tennis slide! or go on afterwards. It is hot enough to roast an ox. What say you?"

"Agreed!"

The young men linked their arms, went a little way out of the town, and then turned down a shady lane. Two gentlemanly young fellows, the senior in rank, though almost the younger in years, was the Rev. Percy Blythe. He had been four years in Langton, was a High Churchman of rather advanced form, and somewhat resented the curb the rector put upon too much zeal in the matter of ritual—the rector being more famed for his common sense than enthusiasm, as regards any extreme views of his curates. Mr. Blythe was a pleasant, hard-working, genial fellow, much given to ladies' society, and much made of generally.

Cyril Dashwood, the second, was a man of good parts as regards his intellect, no great qualities of heart, but intensely ambitious. The son of a man, who had by sheer, hard struggling, made his way from the ranks to a fairly good position in life. This, he thoroughly intended his son should carry on, by means of a wealthy marriage, or fortunate church preferment.

The Rev. Cyril Dashwood was by no means as popular as Percy Blythe, although in appearance, he far surpassed his confrère, for while Blythe was fair, slight, tall, with the kindest of blue eyes, that were always running over with boyish insouciance, Cyril Dashwood was well formed, and his clean, finely cut, if rather severe face, gave the impression that he was descended from, at least, a dozen belted earls, instead of being the son of a Birmingham manufacturer who had staked much upon this aristocratic-looking first born.

" What a strange fellow Lanyon is! What do you think he said this morning ? "

" Something oracular, no doubt," said Mr. Dashwood somewhat coldly. He very often envied the junior curate.

" He said ' If those Brown girls sent him any more of their stupid letters, he would put every one in the fire without opening.' "

" Quite right, too. Those women are perfect nuisances."

" Old Brown isn't a bad sort."

" On the contrary, he is a very good sort, especially without his daughters."

" I believe Lanyon hates all sorts of women. Do you know, Cyril, I fancy he has had some disappointment in that line.

A man does not deliberately dislike women, unless he has suffered some wrong at their hands."

" He is not likely to enlighten us on the subject, you may be sure."

" No, indeed," replied Percy with a laugh. " I could not stretch my imagination so as to imagine *him* discussing such a tender theme ! "

By this time they had reached the junior curate's abode. A pretty, rustic, thatched cottage, with a gay little garden surrounding it. The door stood wide open. A beautiful collie, with soft brown eyes, lay stretched across the threshold, and an old English mastiff watched them coming through the gate with grave friendliness.

" Halloa, Prince ! Well, Rupert, old fellow ! " said Percy, as the dogs came forward to greet him affectionately. " Is your master at home ? " And, escorted by the two dogs, the young men proceeded to find out this fact for themselves, and knocked at a side room door.

"Come in!" a voice called out.

As they entered, there lay the extended form of the junior curate. Round his head was coiled a wet towel.

"Why, Lanyon, what's the matter?" said Percy, with kindly interest in his tone.

"Nothing, only a vile headache. I was out in the sun without my hat—in fact, it fell in the water—and the vaccination combined has touched me up a little. I knew you could get on without me, so made myself comfortable here!"

"The Brown girls, I can assure you, looked quite disappointed. It was bruited about you would put in an appearance this evening."

"If you have nothing better to discuss

than these two young women, please to ring
the bell, and let us have some tea or something."

As the door opened to admit the portly
form of Mr. Lanyon's housekeeper, he
called out:

"Here, Mrs. Bayliss, bring us in some
sherry and soda water; tea, or anything
eatable—stay! Mr. Blythe and Mr. Dashwood will remain to dinner—no, no, tea!"
he corrected, seeing poor Mrs. Bayliss' expression of blank dismay.

"I told Mrs. Bayliss," he continued,
turning to his friends with a smile, "not
to even suggest dinner, unless she wished to
make me ill—so, tea, and anything else you
like to give us."

"Yes, sir," said the woman, greatly re-
lieved.

The room was low-pitched, but roomy,
and very comfortable, with old latticed

windows, set wide open ; and the jessamine and honeysuckle came daintily peeping in, accompanied by a lovely breeze, laden with the perfume of many sweet scented flowers.

Valuable books were scattered about, while the handsome cabinets and chairs hardly tallied with a poor junior curate's salary. But though their junior in rank, he was their senior in age. A man with eight hundred a year, and heir to a baronetcy ! He was a mixture of hauteur and humility, somewhat cold in manner, and, as we have heard, not given to women's influence. A face more conspicuous for power than beauty ; in fact, it was ugly, and only re-deemed by kind, soft, hazel eyes, and crisp, curling hair, too grey to distinguish what its original colour had been. Just now his eyes had a tired, weary look ; indeed, the whole man showed a weariness of body and mind.

His confrères watched him with interest, and if they both held him slightly in awe, and one felt sometimes jealous at what he considered the unfairness of fickle fortune, they liked him much. To them he was as an elder brother. His purse of plenty was for them as for him, and they would have pained him by any refusal or false delicacy. And there existed, as there often does between men, a sincere and unanimous friendship.

"After tea, you fellows, if you will, can do me a service!"

"With pleasure, Lanyon. What is it?"

"Well," he said, pointing with contempt to a basket, "there are a lot of letters, feminine ones, I conclude. I want you to sort them. You know their various hand-writings better than I do Any one that you think looks fresh, or rather, I should say, which is not familiar to you, hand over to me. The others please burn."

"Do you mean to say, Lanyon, you would have us read and destroy your letters without even having seen their contents?"

"That is exactly my meaning. Women's letters do not interest me; indeed I think there is often a good deal of mischief in them."

"But suppose they are business ones?" said Percy, to whom it seemed almost a sacrilege.

"They are not business ones," said the owner of them coldly. "Anyone who wishes to see me on *business* can always do so, except, of course, during these last few weeks. Blythe, my dear fellow, there would not be half so much foolishness going on in parishes if the women were not encouraged to make fools of themselves."

2*

"Come, Lanyon, that's rather strong, to say the least of it," said Mr. Dashwood, with judicial fairness.

"*I* think women quite the nicest half of creation," said Percy, with a laugh.

"Well, I don't," said Mr. Lanyon incisively.

"I think they have their uses," vouchsafed again Cyril.

Mrs. Bayliss here entering with a substantial tea, certainly justified Mr. Dashwood's kind extenuation in their favour. Her bright, good-humoured, motherly face beamed all round.

"I hope your head feels better, sir? I have made you some real strong tea."

"Thank you, Mrs. Bayliss. I am better, and shall enjoy your tea right well."

"That's right, sir. Shall I pour it out, or will one of the young 'gents' here?"

"I'll do it, Mrs. Bayliss," said Percy,

which he did, with deft, practised hands ; and after it was all over Gerald Lanyon lighted a pipe, pushed the obnoxious basket over to his friends, resumed his recumbent position on the couch, and presently seemed absorbed in thought. The rustling and crackling of the letters did not appear to disturb him in the least.

" I say, old fellow, how long, may I ask, have you had these ? There's a precious lot of them ! "

" I should say, a fortnight's collection."

" But suppose they *do* want answers ? "

" Look at the handwriting—settle for yourselves, and go on."

" This one—from ' Jessie Craik '? "

" Tear it up, and either put it in the fire-grate or waste-paper basket ; it is im-material."

" And one from Harriet Brown, and Tilly Brown ? "

"Ditto—ditto, my dear friends."

"Oh, by Jove! here's a pair of slippers, from—from—I can't make out; do you try, Cyril."

"From Matilda Alice Brown."

"So it is."

"Cyril, you can give them away in your district, it's poor enough."

The two young men laughed.

"Suppose Miss Brown comes across them," said Blythe, "what then?"

"If I give her credit for any feelings at all, she ought to be glad; they are useful to an individual who really requires them, and not to one who does not."

"Here is a letter with a crest. The crest looks like that of Lady Wareham."

"I will take that. Lady Wareham is a dear old lady. I am sorry her epistle has been among such . . . frivolous company."

" Here's a new ' fist.' I don't recognise it,
and yet I fancy I have seen it before. It
looks like a man's."

" Read it over," said Mr. Lanyon in-
dolently.

" Miss Higgins presents her compliments
to the Rev. Gerald Lanyon, and having
been informed he requires larger funds for
the Temporary Small-Pox Hospital, on the
Combe Warren land, encloses a cheque
for £200. Mr. Lanyon need not acknow-
ledge the cheque either in writing or in
person.

" Combe Towers,

" July 7th."

" As I do require the funds I shall keep
it, otherwise Miss Higgins might have had
her cheque returned, without thanks."

" All the same, Lanyon, it is a good

thing she *doesn't* require an acknowledgment—it's ten days old, man!"

"Is this the Miss Higgins I hear Lady Louisa so full of?"

"Yes; but you surely know her?"

"I have not that honour."

"By-the-by, of course you don't. She has been in Dresden these last eight months, and you have been here about seven, and nearly a month in quarantine from the civilised world as represented by Langton."

"I am still in ignorance as to particulars beyond the fact that she *is* 'Miss Higgins,' of Combe Towers."

"Miss Higgins is the only daughter and heiress of a deceased 'quack pill' doctor; she is disgustingly rich, very plain, and hates curates."

"So that's it," said Mr. Lanyon, with a laugh. "She *hates* curates."

"She is not quite so bad as Blythe makes

out," said Cyril Dashwood, who had his own views respecting the heiress. " She has a good figure and is considered clever."

" Is she old or young ? "

" About thirty, I believe."

" Now little Esmé Curtis is a darling, if you like ! "

" Is *it* a child ? The *sex* seems doubtful."

" A child ! good gracious ! No ! Miss Higgins has adopted her, and she is about nineteen, eh, Cyril ! "

" Is she disgustingly rich likewise ? "

" No," said Cyril, with a slight blush.

" Poor girl ! "

" Why ' poor girl ' ? " said Cyril with unreasonable irritability.

" To have the ' disgusting riches ' for ever thrust down her throat."

" No, no ! Lanyon," said Blythe warmly, " Miss Higgins is the kindest person to those she likes, and is the most charitable imaginable. It is the curates and those she thinks run after her money that she's so down upon."

"Well, let her rest! Finish the basket off." So they steadily ran through the remainder.

"Here's another parcel! A very handsome birthday book, with some lovely illustrations."

"Percy, old fellow, give that to little Clara Smith, it will amuse her while her poor little leg is 'setting.' I wonder if she would like a doll; or, perhaps, poor little mite, she has had too many babies to drag about to care for anything so childish!"

"She will think a lot of it if she knows it comes from you," said Percy kindly. "But do *you* know who it comes from?"

"Not in the least," answered the other equably.

" It is from Adelaide Craster."

" Well, then, Miss Craster will do a kind action to a poor little waif without knowing it."

" Miss Craster is a nice, lady-like girl. Lanyon, are you not a bit down on these girls ? " said Percy.

" Blythe, believe me, I am not ! I do not ask all these young women to write to me or make me useless presents. On the contrary, I think the whole thing derogatory both to them and to myself."

" Then I suppose you object to tennis because you meet all these girls ? "

" By no means ; tennis is a game all can join in. Personally, I prefer cricket; but, Percy, I think we—nay, I will say *you* fellows, are as much to blame as these girls. How often do you flirt, first with one then another, often looking, if not actually saying, more than you ever intend."

"Oh! they like it, bless you," said Blythe, laughing heartily at the moralising tone of Mr. Lanyon, "*attention sans intention*, you know."

Mr. Lanyon shrugged his shoulders and said no more. He knew his friends thought him straight-laced about many things, but there was so much genuine kindness and goodness about him that they forgave him his little crotchets and heartily respected him.

"Well, Lanyon, old man, we're off now to the Crasters'. We may be in time for a game yet. Can we do anything for you?"

"No, thanks, Cyril," said he as he grasped their hands with warm goodwill.

After the young men had left, he smoked another pipe, and a dreamy, far-away look took possession of his face. He was reviewing a portion of his life, not so very long past, thinking of the young girl he had so idolised almost since childhood. How he had longed and looked forward to the time when he might claim her for his wife! How he toiled and worked and studied! She was the loadstar that drew all his energies to their highest point. How supreme was to be the reward!

And then came the bitter awakening—the soul dragged down from Elysium to an abyss of despair. When Lady Laura Ridden forbade him to think of her daughter, save as the friend of his youth. She had other views for her child. Very soon her mother removed her out of his reach entirely, by marrying the young Pauline to a bilious, elderly millionaire, whose moral character left much to be desired, but the girl made a beautiful sacrifice and centrepiece for his wealth.

Gerald Lanyon never saw his love again. The blow was terrible, crushing in its in-

tensity. The best and purest motives of
his life had failed; his trust was shaken;
what was there to strive for? Nothing!
The lamp had gone out, and nothing but
darkness everywhere. There was no one in
life to comfort him; he was alone with the
apathy of despair.

Then his kind old tutor, who himself had
passed through the furnace, at last gave him
a talisman—to try, in self-sacrifice and devotion to others, to bring back some peace
to himself, so, at length, mounting higher
and higher, gradually the great burden
rolled down. If he had lost the buoyancy
of youth, with all its beautiful illusions, the
endurance of manhood had taken its place,
and now, from the height of his own climb-
ing, he could look down with kind indul-
gence on the shortcomings of those who
were as yet untried in the warfare of life.
And since he had taken "orders" his time and

thoughts found peace in working for others.
And then, too late for his happiness, came
wealth, and the foretaste of possession. By
the death of a young cousin, he found himself heir to an aged uncle, and a rent-roll
of ten thousand a year. So he devoted
himself, and the very liberal allowance he
received from Sir Horace Lanyon, to the
service of others. And now, here he was,
this gracious summer evening, curate of
Langton, not unhappy, somewhat self-con-
tained, but avoiding society as much as
possible.

He rose, shook himself, as if to throw off
this useless retrospection, went into his
room, plunged his head into cold water,
then, calling his dogs, set out with them
for a long tramp through the new-mown
field, scented with fragrant odours, and
delightful with balmy air.

CHAPTER·III.

ABOUT a mile out of Langton was the residence of Miss Higgins, "Miss Higgins of Combe Towers," as she was generally called. It was an old-fashioned place, white, low-storeyed, and somewhat straggling, but capacious and comfortable inside. Outside, Banksias, magnolias, honeysuckle, all in their season, making its old age beautiful, while a few grand old cedars and copper beeches gave it an air of stately dignity. The gardens were perfect, both as to arrangement and in the admirable way they were kept up ; and beyond the gardens were cool green shrubberies planted a century back, affording sheltered walks and pleasant vistas.

The house door stood wide open, and the

evening light was soft and tender, for it had been a golden August day; and now, the air was full of sweet odours, and delicate shadows, cast by the cedars, fell athwart the lawn.

Miss Higgins stood gazing out, and the setting sun glinted her dark hair with warm touches of colour. Her eyes were of deep grey, and the lashes dark: if her cheeks had been tinted with the warm light the sun now gave them, instead of their ordinary sallow tinge, she might have been called a good-looking woman, but there seemed a coldness about her—her mouth, which, but for its sarcastic expression, would have been pretty; the chin was beautifully moulded, soft, round, firm, and yet cleft by a lovely little dimple. Her figure was tall and fine, with a quiet dignity; but with it all, there was a certain something about her which seemed to warn off outsiders, and yet there was often a pathetic look in the grey eyes, a sort of yearning after some unknown possibilities which, as yet, she had not grasped. She was thirty, and she was still Miss Higgins, but it was not for want of offers. Once, indeed, she had nearly loved, but over-hearing some very uncomplimentary remarks *apropos* of her father, her own name, with its want of euphony, and the candid announcement that it was her *money* that was so beautiful in the eye of her would-be suitor, caused a revulsion of feeling which had never as yet been re-versed, and all subsequent offers had seemed to her pained heart but a repetition of the first; she had ceased to believe, but she had courage, and a large-hearted benevolence. Surely there must be some-thing to live for in this great world ! So she accepted her life, only, just this quiet tender evening, with no sound to be heard but the lowing cattle, or the drowsy hum of insects, there did seem an emptiness, a void, in her heart as she stood with her hands idly clasped before her. Then she seemed to throw off these oppressions; for coming down the two or three steps, she called out in clear, rich tones:

"Esmé! Esmé! Where are you, child? Ah," as a smile passed over her face, "in her hammock, of course, wise little maiden."

So gathering her long black lace train over her arm, with light, firm steps, she threaded her way in and out the shady plantation, stopping here and there to gather a flower or a dainty fern, till at last she came to a group of trees, and there under their shade, with little flecks of pink tinted sunshine dancing about her, was Esmé, comfortably reclining in her swing-

3*

ing nest, but not alone, for beside her stood Cyril Dashwood. She made a most dainty and lovely picture. Her sunny hair plaited round a shapely little head, with eyes like turquoise, the eyebrows slightly arched, gave an air of sweet surprise to a baby *mignon* face, with its peach-like fairness.

"What a picture you are, Esmé," said the young man, with passionate, eager eyes, and holding her hand in a tight grasp.

"Do you think so?" she answered, with a happy little laugh. "So do other people, *mon beau monsieur!* There was a German student at Dresden used to follow me like a shadow, till Hester packed him off."

"But you must have encouraged him!" said Cyril, with some heat.

"What is the good of being pretty if you don't make other people feel it? Besides, you forget," she continued, dropping her light tone, " I owe allegiance to no one but dear Hester, and she lets me do whatever I please," but there was an undercurrent of meaning in her voice which was not lost upon Mr. Dashwood.

For months—nay, for over a year—had he been paying her the most devoted attention—in private. He *did* love her deeply, as far as his selfish, calculating nature would allow, and yet it was not her he intended to marry, for he *could* not make up his mind to sacrifice all his ambitious future ; but so contradictory was his temperament that he was wildly jealous of any other man near her.

" And then, Cyril! Why do you love me so much when we are alone, and behave so coldly and ceremoniously when you meet me in society ? It does pain me so. I can't understand it ; it seems as—as if you were ashamed of loving me ! "

"You fancy this, Esmé!" he answered, with some confusion.

She shook her head — for this problem poor little Esmé was always trying to solve.

When Miss Higgins saw the two her face hardened with contempt, and she quickly turned and made her way back to the house and threw herself wearily down on one of the many low easy chairs by the open French window.

"What a wretched set those curates are! Always dilly-dallying after some woman or another! I believe that's all they are fit for."

And her lips curled scornfully as these thoughts flew through her mind. . . . "My poor little Esmé!"

Presently the sounds of footsteps on the gravel outside caused her to look up, and there was Esmé, with a delicious little flush

like a rose-leaf on her cheek, while Cyril
Dashwood had a satisfied smile on his
handsome face that made Hester feel she
almost hated him.

"Hester, I have brought Mr. Dashwood
in. He saw me under the elm-trees and he
wishes to see you."

For a moment her heart stood still.
Was this man, then, going to ask for her
"ewe lamb"? Then she rose coldly and
shook hands, but Mr. Dashwood was not to
be daunted by her hauteur. The prize he
had in view was too valuable not to require
a good deal of patience, besides, he was a
man whom to overcome obstacles was a
pleasure. So, in softly modulated accents,
he told her he came with a message from
the Rector, as Lady Louisa could not come
over herself.

"Thank you ; I heard from Lady Louisa
this morning."

"Indeed! The Rector could hardly have known that."

She made no reply, so he began again :

"But he does want you to become one of the lady patronesses at the cottage flower show."

"Is it money you require, Mr. Dash-wood?" she asked coldly.

"Well, not exactly that, though I dare-say we could do with some more, but it is your presence we want, and Miss Curtis. And there is to be a gigantic tea ; will you undertake something in that way?"

"No, I dislike 'teas,'" she replied in-cisively.

"I think they are rather fun, Hester."

"Well, dear, you can join the tea affair if you like."

"I know the Rector would be so pleased if you would alter your mind and come to the tea. He is anxious all the ladies of influence should be there—Mrs. Grantley will be, and Lady Louisa will preside!"

"Lady Louisa is the Rector's wife, and it is quite suitable she should be *en evidence*, and Mrs. Grantley is the Mayor's sister. I do not intend coming to the tea."

She rose and went to her davenport, and presently returned. "Here is a cheque, Mr. Dashwood, for £25 for prizes; and Hawkins shall send what flowers and fruits you require from the greenhouses."

He thanked her effusively. "You are generosity itself! But you will come, won't you, Miss Higgins?" and he leaned over towards her chair, with a persuasive smile.

"I shall come to the Flower Show. Yes."

And as that was all he could get out of her, he had to remain satisfied. And as she gave him no encouragement to prolong his visit, he reluctantly rose to leave. "Ah! I see fresh fruits of your travels!" and he pointed to some exquisite paintings on porcelain, large in size, and framed in ebony.

"It is the story of 'Undine.' We brought them from Dresden. They excel in those arts."

"And in music?"

"Yes; the music is divine. I think we shall return there soon."

"But surely not this year? You have hardly returned, as it were."

"Probably in the autumn," she answered, in a cold, level voice.

And it was now August. He said "Goodbye" at last, and, as warmly as he dared, pressed her hand, gave a friendly adieu to Esmé, and left them.

"Why can't you like him, Hester?" said Esmé, impulsively. "It is so evident you don't."

" I do not like him."

" But he is so handsome, dear."

" Undeniably so; but *that* is no recommendation in my eyes. Esmé, has he asked you to be his wife ? "

" No——" came hesitatingly from the young lips.

" Then why does he not? You love him, darling."

" Ah, yes, Hester ; indeed, I do ! Perhaps he will." And yet there was a sad depression at the loving heart.

" If he does not, he is using you very badly."

" Oh, Hester ; I can't help thinking——"

" Thinking what, dearest child ? " And Miss Higgins drew the young girl towards her, and with loving, protecting touch, placed her arms round the slender, supple waist. " Thinking what, my little woman ? "

"That—that he loves you better than me!"

"Loves me! Then, indeed, if he does, it's my money bags and my balance at the bank. My dear Esmé, do you think my wits are wool-gathering? *Can* you suppose any man would seek me for *myself?* Come now, look in that mirror! At my ugly yellow face! and yours, like a newly-opened rose! Esmé, God is more just than men. To *you* He has given the Divine power of beauty; to me, in compensation, He has given wealth. I may *buy* homage; but you, darling, can command it. Beauty is an exquisite gift!"

"Hester!" said Esmé, with a loving smile, "You *are* not ugly. Sometimes, when you are moved, your true self shines out. Then you are beautiful! Your colour comes and goes, and then sometimes remains. Your eyes look dark—as dark as the pool where the water-lilies grow! I remember once observing you at the theatre at Vienna. Something in the play deeply interested you; and I thought, 'if others could only see you as I do, they would no longer say my Hester was plain!'"

"You are a most poetical, loving, little flatterer, and therefore your evidence can't be taken."

"Ah, Hester, if you only had someone to love you, you would be like the statue Pygmalion called to life!"

"That is not very likely to happen. Now Esmé, listen to me. It is my intention if any man honestly woos you to settle three hundred a year on you; but I make this proviso, you are not to tell the individual, without my permission; let him love you, dear, for your sweet self. You will promise me this, dear?"

"Oh, Hester! what a noble, loving

heart you have! I don't deserve so much care."

"My dear one, but for you I should become as hard as my own gold. You are the soft spot of my heart. I have neither father, mother, kith, nor kin. You know, dear, how often I have been deceived, in the men who professed *so* much for me. And it is this, perhaps, which makes your love for me so precious. If your Cyril is worthy of you, he won't lose by it; but do not set too much store by his handsome face, it is *not* always the index of a noble mind."

"Hester," said Esmé after a pause, when each was thinking out her own thoughts, "there is such an ugly curate at St. Just. A woman hater!"

"Probably I should prefer him to the others; but do not let us discuss such an unprofitable and uninteresting topic. Let

us rather fly to our music. Play me that
sunny Italian Symphony of Mendelssohn's,
or something of Chopin's. These friends
never disappoint us, Esmé."

~ So Esmé sat down, and under her skilful
fingers Mendelssohn's delicious, sparkling
music brought the bright Italian sky and
the lovely Campagna to their thoughts.
Esmé's one talent was music, and this had
been carefully cultivated at Dresden. She
played with no ordinary skill, and Hester
felt its softening influence. It was like
David's harp, exorcising all the hard
feelings tugging at her heart, and filling it
with tender emotions.

Years ago—when Esmé was a lonely little
orphan, at the same school as the opulent
heiress—had Miss Higgins constituted
herself friend, elder sister, guardian to the
sweet little thing. And as time grew on,
the child's natural guardians were perfectly

willing to resign her to the care of the
wealthy young person who seemed to have
set her heart on this motherless lamb. So
the love had grown between these two,
Esmé slightly selfish, but so bewitching
in her selfishness that one forgave her,
while Hester was touching in her abnega-
tion to the sometimes capricious little
beauty. But the love between them was
deep. Both were orphans, and so clung
together. They had lived mostly abroad,
at Rome, Dresden, Paris, and it was not
often they came to Combe Towers. This
place had been purchased by the Doctor
from an impoverished family, whose dower
house it had been. He had given a
handsome price for it, and spent a good
deal more on what he called improvement,
such as drainage, hot-houses, and other
matters. Part of the old furniture had
been boug' t. But all the beautiful

additions had been made by the cultivated taste of Hester—of contributions from many lands, objects of art and value, some almost priceless.

The old doctor, who had amassed this large fortune by trading on the good-natured credulity of the British public—at least, that part of it who liked senstaional medicine—considerately departed this life, leaving all his wealth to his clever daughter, of whom he stood in awe. But being perfectly certain she would be a safe custodian of all the good things he had gathered together, and of which he was as proud as old David Brown, he had much wished his daughter to carry on his business, but this she declined to do.

"No, father! Let it be ended. I shall have more than enough for myself and others."

"But why, Hester? Why should you

not carry it on? There's nothing I know pays like it."

"Oh, father! I think we have made enough out of the public," and a warm colour came over her face.

"Do you think I've cheated them, eh? Did you ever know any one who died of my pills? My dear, they were as harmless as a piece of paste! It was the *faith in them!* did all the cure. And do you know any reason why people shouldn't get well through faith? And the lovely advertisements! they were the study of my life! All true and original! And look at the enormous good I've done to the artist trade by giving 'em orders for illustrations! My dear, I've been a public benefactor?" And he slapped himself in weak approval, over the region of his heart, for at this time he was near the end of his pilgrimage. "Oh, Hester, if you'd only been a boy! You wouldn't have been so keen about getting rid of a fortune. Perhaps you might marry and have a son? think of *that*, my lass—look to the future."

"No, father dear! Let us be satisfied that we are rich, and, as far as you know, nobody has died." And so it ended, and he likewise—for, leaving everything he possessed to his daughter, he changed his comfortable house for a very grand tomb he had built for himself during his life-time, and on which he carried out his ruling passion, for he drew up his own epitaph; and it was one of the small consolations of his later life to see this grand panegyric of himself as a public benefactor in letters of (highly paid for) gold!

To his daughter this vain egotism was inexpressibly painful, and yet she loved the fond, foolish old man, and tended him with childlike devotion. She felt glad her

4*

young mother, who had died *so* many years ago, long before the pills meant money, and was buried in a humble grave in some Kentish churchyard, did not share this gorgeous mausoleum.

And now Miss Higgins was " a personage," rich, eccentric, not always over agreeable. But she gave liberally whenever money was wanted and therefore merited much consideration at the hands of the town and neighbourhood of Langton.

CHAPTER IV.

In a very charming boudoir in a well appointed house near Eaton Square, sat a very pretty young woman. At least she would have been, but for an expression of utter weariness, discontent and unhappiness. She impatiently tapped her pretty slippered foot, as she listened, or rather did her best not to listen, to the somewhat vehement outpourings of wrath and expostulation, that fell from the lips of a well-preserved woman of fifty, but with this wrath was mingled much anxiety.

"It's no use, mamma! you can't make things any better. I am sick of it all—sick of nearly everything!—of Mr. Cohen and his odious City friends, who I have

to dress up for! and, if it were not for
Charlie Vere, I should go mad, or do
something dreadful. I disliked Mr. Cohen
when I married him, now I almost hate
him! with his cold pompous ways! As if
his money was everything! I think I am
told every week I am a pauper—it is too
much!"

"Pauline! The money *is* a great deal!
What can we do without it? You know
what our life was before your marriage, the
misery of it all—the scraping, the effort to
keep up appearances, and I did try to save
you from it all. I must say you are ungrateful, and a most unloving wife!"

"Mother! If you wished me to be
loving and grateful, you should have let me
marry Gerald Lanyon. I *did* love him!"

"Gerald Lanyon was too poor to keep a
wife. And he had no position."

"Well, he's rich now—directly old Sir

Horace dies, he will be Sir Gerald, with ten thousand a year!

"How could I tell poor young Lanyon would die?" said her mother irritably.

"Of course you could not, but the fact remains."

Lady Laura answered nothing to this, it was too true, and—it vexed her, to think—too late. And her one anxiety now was to try and induce her daughter to make the best of an uncongenial marriage. She had to admit that Mr. Cohen, as a husband, left much to be desired. While his house overflowed with lavish wealth, his wife never possessed one penny she could call her own. She might order what she pleased and run up what bills she pleased—and she did please herself in this last item.

Mr. Cohen had seen perfectly through Lady Laura's tactics. He knew she had sold her daughter. But he was determined his mother-in-law should not benefit by the transaction. He had bought Pauline, like everything else he coveted.

She looked thoroughbred, she was exceedingly pretty, and dainty in her ways. He also found his wife's heart was a commodity that declined to be thrown into the bargain. After his marriage, of course, there were plenty of people to acquaint him with his wife's first love affair. But he consoled himself with the fact that she never saw her old love again.

In point of fact, Pauline was never worth the deep true love of such a nature as Gerald Lanyon's. He had idealised her. She was vain, coquettish, and capricious, perfectly incapable of any depth of feeling; but when happy, she was a charming little personage. But, as she was anything but happy, her charms were absent.

Young Vere had been Mr. Cohen's ward

during his minority, and still made his
home, almost entirely, at Eaton Place.
Wealthy, kind-hearted, not troubled with
too many brains, and, considering all things,
not many vices, he was the *ami intime*
of the house. Mr. Cohen had a real affection for the lad he had had the charge of
for so many years. In fact, he looked upon
him as a sort of " watch-dog," never dream-
ing that Charlie's heart could, by any
chance, become influenced by his capricious,
discontented wife. And this was exactly what
Lady Laura's sharp eyes had discovered.
These two young people, thrown every day
in each other's society, were drifting fast
on a perilous rock. Young Vere was the
daily recipient of Pauline's worries and
vexations —some of them deeply irritating
to a proud, passionate, nature. And pity
was fast merging into love.

" Pauline, dear ! " said her mother, affectionately, "don't have Charlie Vere too much about you! People will begin to notice it, and talk!"

"But, mother! He is his master's watch-dog! and, having an affectionate nature, he naturally loves his mistress!" And the idea pleased Pauline, for she laughed pleasantly.

"Don't joke about it, Lina dear, it is too serious."

"Mamma, pray let me get some amusement out of my life. It is like a prison house with a hateful jailor."

"Pauline! for God's sake *do* try and bear it; it *will* become less hard, if you only would. Oh! if your baby had lived!"

"I am thankful it did not—now. It would only have been a source of unhappiness for me. It is better as it is." And for a moment the young face softened.

The dark eyes were humid with unshed tears, that could at times be so soft and joyous.

"Oh, mother! I found out something dreadful about Mr. Cohen. See! here it is!" And she pulled out from her pocket a much crumpled letter. And her face hardened, as she handed it to her mother. "Oh, it is hateful! But let me tell you how it came into my possession. I am ordered by my husband to get all my dresses made at Madame Stephanie's, and when I was there arranging about one, a fortnight ago, the young person who attended on me (a very handsome girl, mother) had occasion to go to her pocket for a measure, and out fell this letter, and dropped close to me. I picked it up to give it her, when I caught sight of my husband's handwriting. Fancy that! So instead of returning it to her, I put it in

my pocket. Not very honourable, was it?"
she said, grimly; "but all is fair in love
and war. And this is *war!* And there is
nothing like being *au courant* with your
husband's affairs. What do you think of
your son-in-law?" as she saw a trace of
colour pass over her mother's face as
she read the letter.

"Pauline, it is all dreadful. And yet,
dear, hard as my advice must seem to you,
I say bear it. In all these dubious battles
with the world, the woman is *always*
worsted; for even if she is innocent,
'Society' does not stop to judicially ex-
amine. It simply hears of a divorce, or a
separation. 'No doubt the woman was in
fault.' You know in France they always
say, ' *cherchez la femme.*'"

"Mother, I don't care what the world
says. I shall go my own way now."

Just then the door opened, and Cerise,

Pauline's French maid, announced "Mr. Vere."

"Ah, Charlie, there you are! welcome as the sunshine." And Mrs. Cohen impulsively rose, and held out two little white hands, which were eagerly grasped by the young fellow.

The bright dancing eyes, the crisp, curly hair, almost yellow, the pleasant, cheery, sunshiny face, looked the embodiment of animal health and spirits. Small wonder Mrs. Cohen called him her "sunshine."

"Mamma and I are in the dismals; do take us somewhere, Charlie!"

"But where do you want to go, Madamina?"

"Oh, anywhere, as long as it is somewhere," said the young lady inconsequently. "Where do you say, mother?"

"Let us have some tea first, Pauline. But is it quite convenient to Mr. Vere?"

Pauline was highly amused at this idea.

"Of course it is! As if anything I wanted could be inconvenient! What do you say, Charlie?"

"Your wishes are my law," answered the young man, with what Lady Laura considered unnecessary warmth.

"Charlie, just tell Cerise we will have tea at once." Then Pauline went over to her mother, took the letter, and transferred it to her own pocket again, and put her finger on her lips.

"Pauline, I *beseech* you, be careful," whispered her mother, in deep, anxious tones. "It ought to be sent back."

As young Vere entered, Mrs. Cohen asked him if there would be time to drive to Richmond, and yet be back for the theatre. "We might dine there, you know."

"But, Pauline, consider your husband!" exclaimed Lady Laura.

"I don't think he is the least likely to be at home; it is the last week of the session, and he will be at the House, doing his duty to his constituents, who I hope like him better than his wife does."

"Oh! Pauline. *Pray* remember what you are saying. It is most painful."

"Well, mother, don't let's discuss him, then!"

Then the tea, with its etc.'s, came in, and the carriage was ordered for half-past four.

Lady Laura felt it was useless making any further protest. She could only trust that her presence with her daughter and young Vere might lend some degree of respectability to the proceedings. But, nevertheless, she felt sure that they would, had they been so minded, have gone all the same. She saw furthermore that Pauline was getting day by day more intolerant of her husband. Lady Laura sighed sadly; for

she had laid the train herself, and who
could say how and when the match
would be applied? They seemed living over
a mine, which might explode any day.
Should she suggest a word to Mr Cohen as
to the extreme danger of always having
young Vere, like a tame cat, hanging about
the place? It would bring matters to a
crisis! And Pauline would suffer in some
way. No; she felt helpless and hopeless;
affairs must arrange themselves.

Lady Laura had a hard, worldly heart—
which a long life of fighting with adverse
circumstances had not made any the
sweeter, or the advice and snubbings of
high-born relations any the more agreeable.
But to-day, there was an unwonted tenderness in her manner to Pauline. She seemed
now to realize to what a servitude she had
condemned her daughter! She had taken
all her joy from her, robbed her, as it were,

of the love of her girlhood, and given her in exchange chains which she loathed. And this came home to her now with exceeding bitterness. She had intended so much for her child—to place her out of the weary turmoil that springs from lack of means; forgetting that the young wife's heart required a tenderer nourishment than only gold could give. She was but three-and-twenty now; and she had been married four years! Oh, the dreary time! Lady Laura had made every inquiry as to Mr. Cohen's wealth, but very little as to his private character; and now the discovery of this damaging letter had added to the complications. All these sombre thoughts chased each other through Lady Laura's anxious brain. As she watched, almost uncon·sciously, Mrs. Cohen and young Vere amusing themselves in a distant·conservatory, like two idle children, she could hear

Pauline's light laughter, as she threw a handful of rose-leaves at the head of young Vere, which stuck among the wavy curls of his light hair.

Her daughter came in again. " Mother, dear, I am going to put on my things, it's just time." And as she passed out of the room for this purpose, Lady Laura rose from her chair, and quickly went over to where Charlie was standing.

" Mr. Vere," she said, laying her hand on his arm, " Take care of my child."

" Take care of her, Lady Laura! I should think so, indeed!"

" Not only from bodily danger. She is young, thoughtless, and unhappy. Act the part of a *brother*." And she emphasised the word.

A quick, hot blush spread over his face, he understood her meaning.

" I will try!" he answered presently.

"Thank you."

Pauline came in looking brighter, and her dark eyes smiling with expectant pleasure.

"Ready, mother?"

"Put in plenty of wraps, Cerise, and tell your master Mrs. Cohen, Lady Laura and myself have driven down to Richmond."

"Yes, sir. Will Madame be back to dinner?"

"Oh, dear no, Cerise! We are going to dine there," said her mistress.

Oh, the utter blindness—or was it indifference? of the husband, to throw such temptation in the way of these two young people! Lady Laura knew her son-in-law disliked her, and she had seen little of her daughter lately. But events were marching very quickly now. Here was this young man arranging her daughter's movements, taking upon himself the regulation of her

5*

domestic affairs. What *would* be the end
of it all?

"Charlie," whispered Pauline, "I don't
think mamma *can* be well. I believe Mr.
Cohen acts as a nightmare, and weighs
heavily upon her soul. She certainly
seems quite *distraite* and out of sorts, or
perhaps, poor dear, she is bothered about
money affairs. We always were, you know.
And to think I haven't a penny. Isn't it
too bad ?"

"It is," he answered indignantly, "everything is *so* unfairly divided. Here am I
with several thousands lying idle. I *wish*
they were yours, Pauline."

"Never mind, Charlie, the wish is something. Heigh ho !"

"The carriage is at the door, Madame !"

CHAPTER V.

THE Mayor of Langton at this time was a gentleman—a Doctor Lewis—as may be imagined, he was a retired one—with ample means, and a widower, a man about fifty, genial and kind-hearted. What little practice he had now was almost entirely among the poorer townspeople. During this year of his mayoralty his sister, Mrs. Grantley, had come to stay with him. To speak correctly, she was his step-sister—a widow of about four and thirty, tall, striking, not so much on account of her beauty—and she had a fair share of it—as for the bright intelligence displayed in her face. She had very clear, luminous, grey eyes, that expressed every thought and feeling. She was naturally gay and vivacious, independent in thought, word, and deed. As may be supposed, her admirers were many. But between her brother and herself there was a warm attachment. She generally lived in London, but had given herself up this year to Dr. Lewis.

The Red House, the residence of Dr. Lewis, was a handsome, substantial red brick building, lying back from the road, with a charming old garden in the rear. Dinner was over, and they were sitting out on the lawn enjoying the delicious summer evening.

There was the Doctor, Mrs. Grantley, Percy Blythe, Miss Higgins, Esmé Curtis, and Cyril Dashwood.

Dr. Lewis was blowing little graceful clouds from his cigarette, but he was not taking much part in the conversation.

Mrs. Grantley was, and somewhat energetically fanning herself meanwhile. "Indeed I much prefer men to women," she was saying, " not on account of their being especially of the masculine gender, but for their larger and more generous mind; for their greater capacity for fairness. Women generally *are* small minded. They move in a groove, in a flock, like the ' *Brebis de Panurge.*' 'In Society' with them is an unwritten code, stronger than that of the Medes and Persians. I am speaking generally, of course, not individually, for I have known some lovely characters of my own sex! They stand out from the common herd like stars on a summer night. But take your every-day woman! She belongs to a certain set. People who live in large houses, *bien entendu.* It is the house she visits, not so much its inmates, because you hear her so freely pull *them* to pieces! Now would a man care one whit whether his friend lived in a mansion or in a small den

in a back street? Or would he all but cut
him, or give him a cool nod, because he was
not exactly moving in the same sphere?
Not he! but a woman would!"

"Mrs. Grantley! Are you not hard
upon your sex?" said Percy Blythe depre-
catingly.

"No, Mr. Blythe, I am not. I will just
give you a case in point. Some years
back—you will remember Edward?" she
said, turning to her brother, "my father
was able to be of great service in an election—never mind where. The successful
candidate owed a good deal to him, which
he loyally felt. After the election was
over and my father's friend could add the
magic M.P. to his name, he was very
anxious to show some little attention to
my sister and myself, so he desired his wife
to call. She did call, and afterwards we
were invited to a great omnium gatherum

at their house, and then—and there it all
ended. The member's wife grew to be so
short-sighted that we girls often wondered
she did not take to spectacles. We were
only lawyer's daughters! you know. Her
husband was always the same. He would
send us game in the season, or any little
delicate compliment he thought would
please us and our dear old father. After
some year or two I married a gentleman
well known in the London world ; a great
scholar—a *personâ gratia* everywhere. I
happened to meet the wife of the member
for —— at a large ' at home.' She came
forward with some *empressement*, ' I think
I have met you before, Mrs. Grantley ? ' "

" ' I have not the honour of your acquaintance, madam,' I replied, and continued my
conversation with a dear gentle old lady
who *had* known me in my insignificant
girlish days."

"Ah! I do remember *that!*" said her brother with a laugh.

"So now you see why I generally prefer men to women!"

"Perhaps this was an unfortunate selection?" said Mr. Blythe, differing as much as he dared from his goddess.

"It was no selection, it was simply an incident," she answered calmly.

"I think there are a great many sweet women in the world," said Miss Higgins. "I fancy, perhaps, I have found more than men."

"I can agree with you in this, without contradicting my experience. These are *the* ' exceptions,'—which you may meet in all grades of life, from Lady Louisa, who is the truest gentlewoman I know, to the wife of an artisan, who dusts the chair for you to sit upon, as she thanks you for your visit."

"But it is not every woman who can

afford to have the courage of her opinion," said Mr. Dashwood, who had his own ideas of the duties of society.

"I quite agree with you, and that is *why* I prefer your sex. Not perhaps so much *individually*, as collectively," she replied, demurely. "Did not dear old Sir Peter Teazle thoroughly understand the act of malice, when he declined to have his character dissected by the clique at Lady Sneerwell's?"

"Yes, but there were at least three *men* in that *coterie*," said Miss Higgins.

"Oh, my dear Miss Higgins, do you call those creatures men? To my idea, they are sexless. As a woman, I repudiate their mean, contemptible truckling to our worst faults.

'"Nor do they trust their tongues alone,
     But speak a language of their own;
 Can read a nod, a shrug, a look,
     Far better than a printed book!
 Convey a libel in a frown,
     And wink a reputation down!'"

"There's no arguing with you, Mrs. Grantley," said Percy Blythe laughingly.

"No; a woman convinced, you know—"

"What is the point of conviction?" said the Rector, who had just entered.

"Only the superiority of your sex," answered Mrs Grantley, with mischief in her bright defiant eyes.

"That is a gracious admission from the lips of Mrs Grantley," said the Rector, making a courtly, old-fashioned bow.

"Why, dear Rector! Did you ever hear me abuse them?"

"No! But I did not know you admired them."

"I do, very sincerely."

"Then in the name of all my sex, let me humbly thank you, and say—

"'O woman! lovely woman! Nature made thee to temper man: we had been brutes without you.'"

"Well, upon my word, Harry, I could

not believe my ears. You quoting poetry, and what not! What is it all about?" said Lady Louisa, joining the group.

"The Rector is saying something nice about our sex, Lady Louisa," said Miss Higgins, making room for the Rector's wife beside her.

"I am sure I am glad to hear it, because he has often said to *me*:

"' Men have many faults; poor women have but two— There's nothing good they say, and nothing right they do.' "

"Oh, my dear Louisa! that *must* have been *years* ago!"

"Well, it was," said his wife, with a good-tempered smile. "And I am so pleased to think our sex has improved since then."

During this discussion Cyril Dashwood had paired off with Esmé under the shady trees, which prevented them being much

noticed from the drawing-room where the
party had returned. But Hester saw it,
and a vexed look crossed her face and the
resentful feeling against Cyril filled her
heart, and she was not sorry where an hour
later the Rector and Lady Louisa rose to
leave, having to attend a meeting elsewhere,
and asked the Rector to order her carriage
under the plea of a headache; but she felt
a pang of remorse when she saw the tender
light fade out of Esmé's blue eyes and one
of regret take its place.

"I shall take her away to Paris," she
thought—"there will be no rest for us
here."

CHAPTER VI.

THE day of the *fête* had arrived. It was one of those lovely golden days of clear, bright, sunny August. All the Langton world was expected. The Rector, his curates and his wife, were early on the ground to see that every arrangement was as perfect as could be—and it might be as well to say a few words about Lady Louisa, who was a most kind-hearted, good-natured, though important personage, giving herself no airs on the strength of being an earl's daughter, and rather in opposition to her sister, Lady Laura Ridden, who gave herself a great many and not always agreeable ones—for Lady Laura was a disappointed woman, while Lady Louisa, being plain and good-tempered, had received a great deal more than she ever expected. Her husband was kind, considerate, and fond of her. And if he had no particular opinion of her mental capabilities, he had great ones of her heart, for she was one of the kindest and simplest of her sex, and as much liked by the world outside her husband's parish as she was beloved by those in the fold. She was greatly attached to Gerald Lanyon, and equally loved by Hester Higgins. Lady Louisa was one of those rather rare women whose happiness in life consists of little kindly actions to their fellow creatures. She was the very *beau ideal* of a rector's wife. Without fussiness, devoid of pride, with a heart full of sympathy—both for sorrow and joy—a true friend, a thorough woman.

"Louisa, my dear," said the Rector, who had been fussing about for some time. "Have you been into the tea tent? I have been thinking—suppose it rains! Dear me! Is it water-tight, think you?"

"It is not going to rain, Harry, I feel sure. I have not a trace of neuralgia, and you know I *always* have it before rain!"

"I am glad to hear it, my dear! Let us trust your neuralgia will 'bide a wee.' What a splendid show of fruit and flowers have come from Combe Towers! Miss Higgins is a Lady Bountiful!"

"Dear Hester is sure to do her best."

"Miss Higgins gave me *carte blanche* to select what I thought fit from the hothouses, and I am glad you approve of them, Lady Louisa," said Mr. Dashwood with some importance.

The Rector and his wife smiled, and then continued their tour of inspection, and found everything in order.

Nearly everyone had contributed something. The poor, with honest pride, had sent

their very best. There were to be prizes
in money, and articles of vertu for the
more opulent. The ground was gay with
bunting. Under the trees, the gingerbeer
and gingerbread stalls would do a lively
trade. And the band of the local volunteers
would discourse such music as they were
capable of.

Now the company began to arrive. The
Mayor and Mrs. Grantley, who was looking
bright and charming, and the only person
who dared to brave Mrs. Frostick. Mrs.
Grantley was at once the centre of an
admiring throng, the most loyal of her
following being the Rev. Percy Blythe, who
was generally called her shadow.

" I'm afraid we are dreadfully early ; but
the doctor said if he didn't come now, he
couldn't come at all, as he has a meeting
at the Town Hall at four o'clock. Who is
here, Mr. Blythe ? "

"The Rector, Lady Louisa, the Crasters. There are the Brown girls and their father coming in at the gate, and there is Mrs. Frostick in the rear. Lady Laura Ridden is expected, also Sir John Carruthers, from Leigh Marsh."

"Will Miss Higgins be here?"

"Yes, I think so. Is not that her carriage coming over the hill?"

"So it is! Come and let us see some of the flowers and things before the crush. Where is the Doctor? Oh, there he is, with Lady Louisa, in safe company. Where is your woman-hater?"

"Oh, he's somewhere about," said Percy, laughing. "Look! here come some of his foes!" and Matilda Brown, in a pale green dress with a long train, a yellow silk handkerchief loosely knotted round her thin throat, a sort of green-hued 'beefeater' hat with yellow roses, followed by Harriet, in a

6*

white dress, gathered and drawn, and puckered, like a child's, with a pale yellow sash and quilted bonnet with a baby's cap inside, came up with effusion to shake hands with Mrs. Grantley and Mr. Blythe.

"So glad to see you, Mrs. Grantley. Isn't it an awfully fine day, Mr. Blythe? I hope Mr. Lanyon is going to favour us with his company?" asked Miss Brown with some anxiety.

"I believe so, Miss Brown. Here is a friend of yours coming up in full sail," he answered, with laughing malice, as Mrs. Frostick was seen slowly making her way to where they all stood. It was enough for the Brown girls. They firmly believed in discretion being the better part of valour. So Tillie Brown, passing her arm through her sister's, said: "I think, Mrs. Grantley, we will go and see the show. We can do it without crushing now."

" We shall see you again, Mrs. Grantley," said Harriet. " Good-bye for the present."

Mrs. Grantley nodded and laughed, her grey eyes, and saucy little nose, looked the embodiment of mischief.

" I am afraid there won't be a battle after all ! "

" For shame ! Mrs. Grantley," said Percy with a laugh. " Attention ! Here is our friend, the enemy."

" Did you ever see such fools as yon lasses ! Look at them ! " said Mrs. Frostick, as she recovered her breath, and found herself beside the two. " Look at that long rag Tillie's got on ! And Harriet, with a gown that would do for a four-year old bairn ! "

" But they are happy, Mrs. Frostick, and it's a free country," said Mrs. Grantley with a twinkle in her eye. " I daresay you liked to look pretty in your young days."

"Pretty! And you call yon pretty?"

"It's their idea of prettiness! Besides, æsthetic dress is really worn in town."

Mrs. Frostick snorted derisively. "It beats all to see what a soft old fool is David Brown. Why, 'Tillie's thirty-five, come Michaelmas!"

"Mrs. Frostick! do let me put your 'front' straight; it's all awry, and spoils the effect of your toilet," said Mrs. Grantley sweetly.

Mrs. Frostick darted a look of deadly anger at the Mayoress, and with a snort. and a severe clutch at the offending wig, turned abruptly away.

"How could you, Mrs. Grantley?" said Mr. Blythe, convulsed with laughter.

"My dear young friend, you should always hit your enemy in his or her weakest spot. Mrs. Frostick's weakest spot is her false brown front. Here comes Lady Louisa."

"How are you, Mrs. Grantley? But I need not ask! Haven't we a lovely day? Nothing could be better. I do hope everybody will enjoy themselves, especially the children! Their little shining faces are a sight to see. Mr. Lanyon is my especial *aide-de-camp* for the day, so, Mrs. Grantley I give you due warning—you are not to requisition him."

"Now Lady Louisa! That is not fair! Did you ever know Mr. Lanyon desert your colours for mine?"

"Well, no! I will say he is generally faithful. But you are radiant to-day, and armed for conquest; so I tremble for my squire."

"Lady Louisa! Mrs. Grantley has had her first round with Mrs. Frostick, and I am bound to say came off conqueror."

The Rector's wife laughed and shook her head. "Ah! here comes Hester Higgins; I must go and welcome her," but the Rev. Cyril Dashwood was much before her ladyship, for he was ready at the gate to receive the heiress and Esmé as they alighted. Mrs. Grantley's eyes followed them, and an amused smile flitted over her face.

"Which is he after, Percy Blythe?—the substance or the shadow?"

But Percy only shook his head. "I don't tell tales out of school, Mrs. Grantley."

"Then you do know!" said she looking at him keenly.

"Have you been to call on Mrs. Ned Carter, as I asked you?" he asked, instead of answering her question.

"I have, Mr. Blythe! And a very funny person I found her; she asked me to come and 'set' with her as if we were two old hens who wanted to clack! Besides, her whole conversation was on vermin!"

"On vermin? What can you mean, Mrs. Grantley?"

"Exactly what I say! Mrs. Carter complained that her house was overrun with mice, and other odious black creatures. So I faithfully promised—in *your* name—a cat and a hedgehog!"

"How could you? Where am I to get a hedgehog?"

"I have not the faintest idea. But I wil suggest this much, if you want me to look her up you really must provide her, every now and then, with some fresh topic of conversation, for I came away creepy to a degree. Now let us go and see those orchids of Sir John Carruthers'; I hear they are wonderful."

CHAPTER VII

In the meantime Miss Higgins and Esmé were walking about with Lady Louisa, Cyril Dashwood firmly attaching himself to Hester, and hardly noticing the young girl so much as by a look; indeed, he seemed almost studiously to avoid her. And yet Esmé had hardly looked fairer—so dainty and fresh was she—in her soft pale dress of blue and her damask roses. She tried to put a bold face on this cold desertion, but her heart was wounded to a degree. So she turned her pretty face to Sir Ernest Beldon, who had just joined the group. A well-to do young country squire, whom they had known abroad. And was only too happy for Esmé's attention at any price, as he was wildly in love with her.

"Miss Curtis! do let me escort you

through some of the tents. They are quite worth a visit."

"I shall be very pleased to go! Where shall we find you, Hester?"

"Never mind, dear, just for an hour. I shall be sure and see your blue frock and your red roses," said Hester, only too glad to have her dear child away from the torment she knew she was suffering. So Esmé, without one glance at Cyril Dashwood, passed out of sight with her handsome young squire.

"Come with me first into the tea tent, Hester, dear. I think Mr. Lanyon is there. You will not mind if he is not particularly polite or attentive. In fact he dislikes ladies' society. But he is such a kind, good fellow. If you only could know *what* he has been to those poor wretched gipsies! They are down with small-pox, and have given no end of trouble. He has managed to get a temporary hospital for the poor creatures—it is only a rough wooden affair, but contains a good many comforts for them. And really until he took up the thing it was *most* serious. The Town Council feared they would bring infection into the town. But, however, he, and Dr. Macartney from London, between them, have done wonders. Absolutely got them to have their children vaccinated. He has arranged for provisions being conveyed to them. So they, on the whole, are really getting better now, thanks to his noble self-denial. His own vaccination has made him wretchedly ill. You haven't met him at all, my dear? Gerald Lanyon is not the least good-looking, though I hear the young ladies *would* make a lot of him if he would only let them. The fact is, dear, he is *very* well off," said her Ladyship, slyly, "for a curate."

Mr. Cyril Dashwood, finding his company almost ignored by the two ladies, took himself off, and rather regretted he had not paid more attention to Esmé. However, there she was, walking about, apparently enjoying herself, with Sir Ernest Beldon. While he was wandering aimlessly about, with something like a scowl on his handsome face, he was waylaid by Miss Matilda Brown! It was all in vain he pleaded anxiety to find the Rector. She knew " the exact spot where the Rector was located." Inwardly he anathematised her; but it was all no good. Miss Brown was not to be parted with. She was impervious to his cold, abrupt answers. She had found an escort, and did not mean to let him go.

In the meantime Lady Louisa and her companion had reached the largest tent on the ground, gaily decorated with flags. Several children were running in and out.

"Oh, children! children! You ought not to be here till tea time, and it's not *near* that!"

"If you please, my lady, we ain't touched nothing. Mr. Lanyon said we might, if we didn't meddle with anything, and we haven't, my lady."

"Very well," said my lady, good-naturedly. They were the children of her own Sunday school class, and somewhat spoilt.

"Lady Louisa! you must scold me," said Mr. Lanyon, coming through the opening and answering for himself. "I told them they might stay, and they have been helping me to put some flowers about that Mrs. Bayliss has just sent in! And now you can run away, youngsters," he said, turning to the children.

"Dear Hester! will you let me introduce Mr. Lanyon to you, and make acquainted

two dear and valued friends?" Nothing
could be happier than Lady Louisa's
manner, to make it, as it were, a
personal favour to herself, that they
should be good friends. She knew the
bristling crotchets on both sides.

Mr. Lanyon came forth and shook hands.

"Miss Higgins, I have to thank you very
deeply for your kindness to some rather
unhappy friends of mine at Combe
Warren."

"Pray do not thank me, I am only too
glad to be of any service. And they are
on *my* land! Besides, I consider it part
of a debt I owe."

He looked enquiringly at her.

"I mean," she answered with almost a
defiant blush, "that as most of my money
comes from the public, it is but fair they
should have some of it back again."

"Any way, it has been most useful,"

he replied simply: "it enabled me to engage another nurse, and other requirements."

"I am so *glad* of that, do please draw on me for anything you want; food, comforts of any kind. You will, will you not?" she asked eagerly, her face lighting up with earnestness.

"Indeed I will, and at once claim your kind help. First, will you let your housekeeper make a good quantity of strong beef-tea, and any other kitchen physic you will suggest. And if one of your men will leave it twice a week at Combe Hill, by the sign post, some one from our border land shall come and fetch it; and if you would send it in some old jars which need not be returned, your servants will stand in no fear of infection. It will be a great help to us."

"It shall be done, and at once, and

I will send word directly the first consignment is ready."

"I thank you much, and I trust it will not be for long, so many are convalescent; but it is just they who require the more help, to get quite well."

"Do you not run some risk yourself?"

"Just a little perhaps, but I have been vaccinated and gone through the process of quarantine, and now, with the extra nurse and Dr. Macartney, I am going to give to myself a holiday and look after them at a distance; and independently of all this, I have neither father, mother or wife, so you see my health is of no serious importance to anyone."

"Gerald, you are ungrateful to say so," said Lady Louisa, reproachfully.

"Forgive me! dear friend," he said quickly, turning towards her. "I *am* ungrateful."

Miss Higgins looked at him with some interest—at the square, rugged face, over which flitted the softening shadows of kindly feeling. No, he was not like the curates it had been her luck to come across. There was no effeminacy about him—he seemed always to have mixed with the strong, and to have retained their strength.

On his part, he was surprised; he was not prepared for this earnest, refined woman. This was no purse-proud heiress, but a human being full of kindly sympathies. And most certainly she was not plain! Plain! What a strange delusion! With those beautiful deep grey eyes, and that changing expression.

Just then, Cyril Dashwood entered, none too pleased to observe the friendly intimacy that seemed to have sprung up between Miss Higgins and Lanyon; he likewise noted the eager animated face of

Hester, it had never beamed upon him like that, it positively made her decent-looking! And then—when she turned and saw who was the intruder, her face resumed its usual cold sarcastic hauteur.

"Lady Louisa! they are seeking you everywhere. Lady Laura has arrived!"

"Lady Laura!" mechanically exclaimed Gerald Lanyon.

"Oh, Gerald, dear! I forget to tell you she was coming, but you need not see her."

He made no remark, but his face was pale and stern.

Lady Louisa turned to the others.

"Well, I suppose I must go, but it is very pleasant here. Will you come, Hester, or remain here till I come again?"

"I will remain—it is quiet and cool."

"I will rejoin you, Miss Higgins, in a few moments," said Mr. Dashwood, reluctantly leaving them.

Miss Higgins vouchsafed no reply. But she had marked the quick look of pain on Mr. Lanyon's face, and turned to address some observation to the children, who were again at the tent door, and so left him to recover himself.

Then Mrs. Grantley put her bright face in.

"Ah, there you are, Miss Higgins! Miss Curtis was looking for you. But, I may add, she is well cared for, Sir Ernest Beldon is showing her all the lions of the show."

"I am so pleased to hear that," said Hester.

"I hope I have not scared Mr. Lanyon away, but, even while I was speaking to you, he glided past me, like a substantial ghost," said Mrs. Grantley.

"I expect he is required in a good many places."

" What a pity he is so churlish!"

" Now, Miss Higgins, will you make the tour of the grounds under my guidance?" said Mr. Dashwood, who had just returned, breathlessly anxious to give no quarter to Gerald Lanyon. "I consider myself the master of the ceremonies, to a certain extent."

" Thanks.—No! Mr. Dashwood. I have seen a good deal already, and am comfortable here," and she spoke with such provoking coldness, that he almost hated her, while Mrs. Grantley's demure face was a study.

" Do please come, Miss Higgins! I want you to see Hawkins' contribution, on your behalf."

" Very well. Come, Mrs. Grantley, shall we start then."

" With pleasure," answered that lady, with a little twinkle of her eye. She knew this was the last thing Cyril wanted; so she just whispered in his ear: "Two's company, three's none, eh, Mr. Dashwood?"

He frowned angrily, but said nothing.

So presently his tormentor said: "Find me Percy Blythe—I'll be bound he is not very far off—or the Doctor. No! not the Doctor! he will want to be going, and I mean to stay and see——all the fun! It's no good, believe me, dear Mr. Dashwood!"

Cyril reddened angrily, but he knew it was useless fighting with Mrs. Grantley. In the first place she would not care, and would rather enjoy it, and on the whole she was too nice to quarrel with. Presently, to his great relief, he saw Percy Blythe ahead of them.

"Here, Blythe! Mrs. Grantley has been wanting you these last ten minutes. Do come and make yourself useful!"

Mrs. Grantley only shook her head,

while Cyril profited by the diversion to walk on in front with Miss Higgins.

"My dear Percy, Cyril Dashwood has been in agonies. He wanted to get rid of me a quarter of an hour ago. It was a bad quarter, you may guess. And to think he is throwing all the pearls of his eloquence away on the lady! See! she doesn't even listen to him. Why don't you tell him he is playing a losing game? He is sacrificing Esmé, who is soft enough to care for him, for Hester Higgins, who despises him down to the ground. Why don't you say something?" she asked impatiently. "Are you dumb?"

"Dear Mrs. Grantley, please don't be hard on me. A man should be loyal to his friend. And would my interference be judicious? On the contrary, it would be almost impertinence."

"You are right, Percy, forgive me!" and

she put out a dainty little gloved hand, which he warmly grasped.

Under his pleasant, debonair exterior, he had a loyal, upright heart. Mrs Grantley was to him a woman among women. No girl would ever appear so charming, and yet he knew she would never love him. No! as far as he was concerned, she was unattainable. She might tease, command, vex him—all which she did within the twelve hours of the day—but still, he would rather have her friendship than another woman's love.

Mr. Lanyon had disappeared. Lady Laura Ridden and her sister were walking about absorbed in earnest conversation.

"Laura! if you ask Gerald Lanyon to undertake such a task, it would be right down cruelty ; nay, it would be *bad taste*. You have embitttered his life almost past recovery. Can't you leave him alone now?"

"Louie! drowning men catch at straws. So that I could save Pauline, I would not care who was sacrificed. What is Gerald Lanyon to me, that I should consider him, if he can serve my turn? It is useless now to say: 'Why did I not let her marry him years ago?' How was I to tell young Horace Lanyon would be killed on a Swiss mountain? I wish now, with all my heart, she had married him, but wishes will do no good," and Lady Laura sighed deeply. "Pauline told me plainly yesterday, if Charlie Vere would take her away, she would elope with him. I have absolutely nothing but young Vere's honour to cling to, for she has found out some things about Mr. Cohen's private life, and now she is reckless!"

"It *is* terrible, Laura dear," said her

sister, with a world of sympathy in her tones.

"Well, don't let us talk any more now," said Lady Laura abruptly. "People will think we are plotting. Who is that rather *distingué* looking woman walking across there, with one of your curates—in black and amber?"

"Miss Higgins."

"What! that old quack's daughter?

"Yes."

"Good gracious! What a pity I have no son, or that yours is a boy at Eton. She is so rich!"

"My dear Laura, Hester Higgins is much too good to be sacrificed to anybody. I have both great love and great respect for her. She is not a woman to be easily won. I am much attached to her."

"My dear Louisa! You always have been attaching yourself to somebody or

something all your life! I believe a harmless snake would not come amiss!"

Lady Louisa was not in the least dis-
turbed by these sarcasms. Had she not
endured them for many years of her life?

"I daresay you are right, Laura; I don't
profess to be as clever as you, dear. But
with regard to Hester I know and feel there
is something good and great in her, and if
she *does* marry I hope it will be to some
good man, who will love and value her for
herself, not her money—she is far above
rubies."

"My dear Louie, you are getting poetical? I am practical! Introduce me to
your paragon."

"As soon as they come this way I will."

"Are those some of your local 'celebri-
ties?'" asked Lady Laura, putting on her
eyeglass and carefully examining Tilly and
Harriet Brown, who happened to cross her

ladyship's point of sight, in eager chase of
Mr. Blythe, whom they eventually caught
up. And he, far too gentlemanly and kind-
hearted to cause them mortification, stayed
and chatted with them ; and this too in the
sight of Mrs. Frostick !

" They are two Miss Browns, and they
have a nice old father."

" I see !   He balances the daughters ! "

By this time Hester, attended by the
faithful Cyril, approached the two ladies.

" Hester, dear ! My sister would much
like to make your acquaintance."

" I shall be very happy, Lady Laura ! I
met your daughter, Mrs. Cohen, last year
at Homburg—"

" Did you, really ? "

She was with the Mountchesneys.
They were all staying at the same hotel."

Lady Laura frowned. These same Mountchesneys were as much her *bête noir* as

Charlie Vere. Lady Louisa came to the
rescue.

"Did you not think my niece very pretty,
Hester?"

"Indeed we did! She was so much
admired at Homburg—"

Then, to his great chagrin, Mr. Dashwood
was called away. He liked being associated
with the Rectory party. Nevertheless he
felt he was making but little headway with
the heiress. All he could get out of her
were monosyllables, and she seemed bored
to death. And all this time a hot unreasonable anger against Esmé possessed him,
who appeared to be entirely engrossed by
the young baronet and forgetful of *his*
presence. He could not understand that the
young girl, bringing pride to the rescue
of her wounded feelings seemed far more
interested in young Beldon than she really
was, for her heart was very sore. The

whole time she had been there *her* Cyril had devoted himself, pointedly and absolutely, to Miss Higgins. What right had he to love her (Esmé) and then to devote himself to another woman?—it was too cruel! And it was only with great difficulty she could restrain the tears from overflowing the tender blue eyes—they were in her heart. The afternoon to her had been a miserable failure. What matter that she looked lovely, that her dress was beautiful? Cyril did not notice it! Why should she suffer so? Ernest Beldon had left her for a moment to go and procure some ices, when Hester came and sat beside her.

"Esmé, love! Lady Louisa wishes us to go to the Rectory and spend the evening there, instead of going back to dinner."

"Oh, Hester! I wish we were going home."

"Why, dear? Haven't you enjoyed yourself?"

"Don't ask me!" she answered tremulously.

"Would you like to go home now, darling?" said Hester tenderly.

"Oh, Hester! Would you? You are not vexed?"

"Vexed, love! How could I be? Shall we have the carriage? I do not care to stay."

"Are you quite, quite sure, Hester?"

"Quite, quite sure!"

Sir Ernest Beldon came up to them with two plates of ices. "I have one for you Miss Higgins! I saw you sit down."

"Thank you, Sir Ernest! And after we have consumed them, will you kindly order my carriage?"

"Order your carriage! Oh, surely you are not going yet?" he exclaimed in tones of such evident disappointment that Hester felt quite sorry for him.

"I think we are both tired, and Esmé has a headache."

"I am so sorry! I fear it is all my fault"—and he looked anxiously at Esmé, who looked pale and weary — "dragging her about all this broiling afternoon!"

"Please don't say so!" said Esmé feeling some reproach, as she saw the kind honest face of the young man clouded over with disappointment. "You have been so kind to me."

"Sir Ernest! I hope you will find your way over to the 'Towers,' said Miss Higgins heartily. "Indeed, I shall be glad of your advice about some land I think of buying!"

"I shall only be too glad!" said he, visibly brightening, and he registered a

vow of mental gratitude to the kind owner
of Combe Towers.

So with these thoughts to cheer him he
went in search of the carriage.

Miss Higgins went to make her excuses
to Lady Louisa, and Cyril Dashwood came
up hastily to Esmé.

" What is this I hear about your going ? "
said he roughly.

" Simply that we are going," she replied
coldly.

" What ever for ? I have not spoken to
you all the afternoon ! You have been so
taken up with that idiotic young prig,
Beldon ! " She made no answer.

He felt irritated that Esmé, usually so
docile, so submissive to all his selfish
whims, should even by silence resent any
mood he chose to indulge in.

" Come Esmé! I suppose you are
offended ? "

"Pray, do not think so, Mr. Dashwood!"

"Mr. Dashwood! So that's it!"

Then the Rector, Lady Louisa, and Sir Ernest Beldon came up.

"I think you are both most cruel!" said her Ladyship to Esmé—who looked so sad and penitent that Lady Louisa stooped down and kissed her. "However I shall come over and see you to-morrow."

"I see the carriage at the gate; come Esmé!" and Hester, with the Rector and his wife, walked on, while Ernest Beldon kept close to Esmé, notwithstanding that Cyril Dashwood, with scowling brow, was on the other side of her; and as the young baronet handed her into the carriage he leaned over and softly whispered (but not so softly that Cyril's jealous ears caught it)—

"I will send for that book as soon as ossible, and bring it over."

Cyril looked enquiringly at Esmé, but

she made no sign, and the carriage drove off.

The Rev. Cyril Dashwood walked apart by himself, with anger and jealousy tugging at what did duty for a heart. Esmé went up considerably in his estimation. The very fact that someone else admired her sought her—— "Good heavens! I *have* been a fool this afternoon! Wasting my ·time on that mass of iron and ice! While Esmé—— But still! What is the use of her, poor little darling! Sunbeam as she is! Without a sou! No! I must still work at that odious fortress of a woman— how I shall hate her when I do succeed!"

You see the Rev. Cyril Dashwood had a profound belief in himself; he only imagined it was a work of time with the obdurate, hard-hearted heiress. Failure, he could not understand.

Once out of the turmoil, and on the road

home, Esmé's self-possession gave way, and
the pent-up tears coursed each other down
her pale cheeks. "What is it, darling?"
said Hester.

"Oh, Hester! Hester! I am so unhappy;
it has been such a wretched afternoon, and
I had so looked forward to it!"

"Poor child! I think I can guess," said
the elder woman, with infinite tenderness.
Oh, Esmé! what things we women are!
We lavish the precious gold of our affection
on such worthless creatures. There is good,
honest, Ernest Beldon, who worships you,
and yet your eyes are so blinded by that
insufferable, self-seeking, selfish young man,
Cyril Dashwood, that you can't see it! I
have the most supreme contempt for him."

"Hester, I see all his faults, and I see
Ernest Beldon's goodness. And yet I can't
help it. Do we not almost love their faults
when they are part and parcel of the beloved

object? I love Cyril. Don't despise me, Hester," said Esmé, humbly.

"Despise you, my darling! Not that, indeed! How can you help your tender heart of nineteen——? And yet! The pity of it——"

"Have you ever seen Ernest Beldon's home at Heminglee?" presently asked Miss Higgins.

"No."

"It is such a sweet place! It is part and parcel of an old Priory. I remember going there some years ago when Lady Beldon was alive. It must be dull for him, poor fellow, now that his sister has married."

"Who did she marry?" asked Esmé with languid interest.

"Sir Percy Willis."

"Oh, then we met them last year at Mrs. Munroe's."

"Yes. Do you not remember saying she

was the prettiest and best-dressed woman there?"

"Yes! She wore white velvet and pearls."

"And I think she is so like her brother, with just the same winning expression," said Hester, with sly unconsciousness of tone.

"Hester, did you see Mr. Lanyon?"

"Yes. He was in the large tea tent."

"Well?"

"Well, little curious, for a curate he is very sensible."

"Do you think him so ugly?"

"I can't say—No!—I think he seems much in earnest."

"Was he so very disagreeable?"

"Not in the least."

"Oh Hester!" said Esmé, returning to her own troubles again, "Why did you keep Cyril all the afternoon?"

"Keep him! Surely, you cannot imagine

I wanted such an insincere, conceited person attached to me! His presence was a perpetual blister. Any other man but himself would have had too much tact, too much dignity, to have persisted in such attentions. I can only conclude he considers himself some sort of an official at the show, and as I was rather a large contributor, merited large attention; and if I ever waste one thought upon him, it is with regret for you, dear. For myself, I despise him," and Miss Higgins's face left no doubt of her meaning.

"My dear, it strikes me, he will soon find out he can't run with the hare and hunt with the hounds. Now, here we are! and there is old Major barking a welcome. There's no place like home, is there, Esmé?"

"No, darling! And no one like Hester," said the girl, giving her a fond hug.

CHAPTER VIII

The next day, Lady Louisa and her sister, Lady Laura, drove over to Combe Towers to lunch. Lady Laura had no objection whatever to cultivate the friendship of a rich, independent young woman ; poor people, in her eyes, were the greatest of mistakes. She was charmed and impressed by everything. The complete, though subdued effect of wealth, rather felt than seen, the perfectly appointed household, the gracious, calm, dignified hostess, clever if sarcastic, but always well-bred. She remarked almost with envy, the affection that seemed to subsist between her homely sister and the heiress. While to Esmé, Lady Laura considered Miss Higgins's affection absurd. A companion ! and to be treated more like a spoilt child; petted and humoured, and consulted as if she were a person of consequence. Even her sister was almost as bad; but then, no one ever expected any sense from Louisa!

What a thing it would be if she could induce Miss Higgins and her wayward Pauline to become friends. How might not that clever, cold, clear-headed woman, influence the excitable, frivolous, and certainly unhappy wife of Mr. Cohen! It was well worth working out—so she formed a resolve, but said nothing to her sister about it.

After luncheon, Lady Louisa asked Hester if she would drive back to Langton with her, for about an hour or two.

" The fact is, Gerald Lanyon, not satisfied with his hospital at Combe Warren, is anxious to try and get up a permanent one at Langton. A sort of cottage hospital.

You know we have nothing of the kind, and have to send all our cases to Barrington, twenty miles off ; but it will be rather up-hill work, and I must say the Rector is not over keen about it. He says he can't see *where* the money is to come from. The townspeople *may* take it up, but they are just as likely to say they have done without it all these years, and their fathers before them, and why should they have one now ? They are most kind and good, but they are not progressive."

"Dear Lady Louisa, I need scarcely say it will have my warmest sympathies. Indeed, I think it is one of the privileges of wealth, to help and succour those who lack it."

"Gerald Lanyon seems to have a craze on hospitals," said Lady Laura, coldly. From the time I arrived yesterday, I have heard of nothing else, except indeed small-pox, by way of a cheerful variety, I suppose."

" Yes, but dear, Gerald thinks so much suffering might be prevented by timely attention and care."

Lady Laura shrugged her shoulders ; she was utterly bored by it all.

" Suppose we begin at once," said Miss Higgins, with some eagerness. "If Lady Laura will do me the pleasure of remaining as my guest, during my absence for two or three hours, Esmé will be my representative. I think the conservatories will repay a visit."

" Nothing will give me greater pleasure. I am anxious to inspect all your valuable curiosities, I have heard so much of them."

" They are all at your service, Lady Laura."

The two friends then drove off.

"Hester, I don't think I ever told you why Gerald Lanyon is so dear to me, almost as my own son. In the first place, his dead mother was my earliest and dearest friend, and, my dear, he has been the victim of my sister's worldliness. He had grown up with Pauline, my sister allowed them to be thrown together with the most perfect indifference, and, of course, they loved each other. He passed with high honours at Cambridge, and was reading for the Bar, but he was poor, nothing much but his own brains to rely upon. So things drifted on, he always loving pretty, foolish Pauline, until one day, he asked Laura for her daughter's hand, so soon as he should have made a start in life. My sister was amazed, and suddenly making up her mind, distinctly forbade any such idea— separated them, by carrying Pauline to London, and within a year married her to

Mr. Cohen. Anything more unhappy than that marriage, can hardly be imagined."

" Have they never met since ? "

"Never! It went badly with poor Gerald, he had brain fever. After many months, our dear old friend Dr. Berners, advised him to take orders, with a conviction, that, in interesting himself in others, he would forget his own griefs."

" And has he done so ? "

"I think he has to some extent, but he is very reserved. I wish he could meet with some woman who could, and would, undo the mischief my sister and Pauline occasioned. He has a noble heart, but I feel convinced that Pauline would never have made him happy, she is so trivial, nay, almost childish, to say nothing of her caprice. She certainly is a dainty, fascinating little thing, but a man with a disposition like Gerald's, with so much craving

after a nobler and higher life, requires
something better than mere prettiness.

Now, it must be confessed that Lady
Louisa, in that commonplace head of hers,
was hatching a scheme, which she, in her
turn, intended to keep to herself, and this
was to raise a feeling of warm friendship
between Hester Higgins and Gerald Lanyon.
She knew they were both people with
' corners,' but still, " *On guérit comme on
se console ; on n'a pas dans le cœur de quoi
toujours pleuter, et toujours aimer.*"

So she trusted in her own diplomacy,
that what began in mutual interest and
friendship, their own hearts would one day
finish. Lady Louisa was aware that
Hester disliked clerics, therefore she merely.
interested her sympathies in " the man "—
not the curate.

"I do not wonder he dislikes women-
kind after that," said Hester after a pause.

"My dear, we will drive on to Mr. Lanyon's cottage, because he has all the plans there." As they drove down the pretty lane they saw the gentleman in question about to enter his gate, but hearing the sound of wheels he turned as the carriage pulled up. He seemed surprised—Miss Higgins thought, to see *her* with Lady Louisa—and not over pleased.

"We are coming in, Gerald. Miss Higgins will lend a gracious ear to your cottage hospital plan—if you take her while she is in the humour." Hester smiled, and Gerald held out his hand to assist the ladies to alight.

" Go in, please, Lady Louisa, while I get my man to put up the ponies," for Lady Louisa and her friend had dispensed with that sometimes inconvenient third—a manservant.

" *What* a cosy room, Mr. Lanyon!"

" I am glad you think so, Miss Higgins, as much of its cosiness comes from my dear friend here."

" I do ' mother ' him occasionally, Hester."

" Occasionally ! Always ! dear friend."

Hester thought his face so pleasant as he turned in animation to the Rector's wife.

Then he and Hester fell to discuss the plans, and anon a bright eager light came into the grey eyes, so full of intelligence and kind womanly feeling, that Gerald threw off his reserve and plunged into details *con amore.* Lady Louisa, placidly seating herself in a comfortable armchair near the open window, produced from a reticule a quantity of homely knitting, and with a very satisfied expression set to at her work. The bees came droning in. The odours from the flowers sent in a fragrant breeze, the tall sunflowers threw long shadows, the holyoaks bent gently to the whisper of the wind ; Prince, and Rupert, lay stretched in the sunshine, and gradually Lady Louisa's fingers relaxed ; there came a gentle murmur of voices from the far end of the room, and with a pleasant little sigh the Rector's wife closed her eyes—and then she slept.

The two talked on. The shadows grew longer. Mrs. Bayliss brought in some tea. Lady Louisa opened her eyes ; surely she must have had a few minutes' doze ? Then Hester poured out the tea, and Gerald handed it to her. "I think we see our way, dear friend," said he. "I cannot thank Miss Higgins enough."

"I am so glad it is in train," said her Ladyship, with demure quietness, "I thought your two wise heads would manage it."

The old housekeeper came in again to know if the ladies would like any fruit, and was supremely happy when Lady Louisa expressed a wish to go and see her chickens.

Then Gerald produced all his treasures for Hester's inspection, and she in return begged him to come over to Combe Towers and see hers—brought from many countries. He willingly acquiesced; indeed he felt refreshed when he looked into those clear honest eyes. "I shall come," he said, and clasped her hand warmly, " and thank you deeply for your interest in my work!"

"Shall we say our work, Mr. Lanyon? Poor humanity is not exclusive."

"Be it so," he answered with a smile.

Lady Louisa entered. "Hester! Your ponies are anxious to be off, and the Rector will be scolding me—he does sometimes, you know, dear man!"

Hester felt a strange new feeling of plea_

sure, which she could hardly analyse. It seemed like some wave of gladness that hitherto had never before visited her. True, it was only one of her many acts of charity! And yet, was it a ray of this pleasant evening sun that was shining in her heart? She knew not—but there was a brightness in everything.

"Well, my dear, will you send Laura back? You must let one of your men bring her home," said Lady Laura, as they drew up at the Rectory.

Hester started! "Of course, dear friend, I will see to Lady Laura's comfort and convenience. Oh, dear Lady Louisa! I have spent such a pleasant afternoon," said she kissing her friend with all Esmé's impulsiveness. And the Rector's wife said nothing, but kissed her affectionately in return. And then her ladyship got down and watched the carriage drive off with its

9*

solitary but happy occupant. Then she
nodded her head, and a comfortable smile
spread over her face : " Bless the dear
creatures ! They are made for each other !
But I wouldn't have Laura know it for the
world ! "

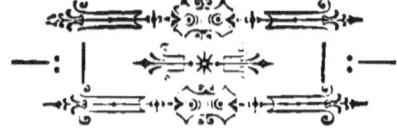

CHAPTER IX.

Mrs. Cohen and her maid Cerise were in deep consultation, and the young lady was pacing restlessly up and down, her pretty pale blue *robe-de-chambre* flowing in long graceful folds round her.

" Isn't it time he was here, Cerise ? "

" *Mais non!* Madame ! it wants half-an-hour yet."

" Oh dear ! I wish he would hurry ! Mr. Cohen may come home any moment, and the man not clear off." And she stopped her restless walk to listen eagerly.——Then presently a knock was heard, and Cerise went out.

" It is the young man from ' Storr and Lazenby,' " whispered Cerise, entering with a young man, who held a small parcel in his hand.

" We have executed your order, Madam, and you would hardly know the paste from the original. Messrs. Storr and Lazenby have given seven hundred for the necklace, and the cost of the paste imitation is fifty pounds. I have the seven hundred with me and shall require your receipt."

" Only seven hundred ! Why it cost a thousand ! "

" Doubtless, Madam ! but buying and selling are not exactly the same."

" So I perceive ; however, I will take that."

" Here is the receipt, Madam, if you will be so good as to sign it—just there. And here are the notes " (and he took from an inner pocket a pocket-book and counted out the fresh crisp notes, and a smaller bag with sovereigns) "and the gold as you directed. Will you be pleased to inspect the paste necklet and see if it meets with your approbation." And then from the parcel he produced the sparkling necklace.

" Oh that is exact! isn't it, Cerise ? "

" It is Madam ; it is perfect ! *Tiens !* " she whispered hurriedly—" I hear monsieur arrive in his dressing-room, he has just rung his bell ! "

" That will do, thank you," said Pauline, as she hastily signed the receipt and dismissed the man. Then she swiftly swept off the gold and notes into an escritoire, locked it, and put the necklace into her jewel box. She had only just accomplished this, when a knock was heard at her dressing-room door beyond the boudoir ; the rooms led out, one into the other. She rapidly crossed the two rooms and opened the door—it was her husband !

" What! not dressed yet ! it is nearly eight o'clock ! "

"I shall not be long," said Mrs. Cohen, with unwonted amiability. "I will ring for Cerise now."

"Pauline! you will wear your diamonds to-night."

"I was going to wear pale blue and pearls."

"Well then, wear something else and diamonds," with that, he closed the door.

"Can he have heard?" she asked eagerly of Cerise, who was in the farther room, as she listened nervously to the departing footsteps of her husband.

"No, no, madame, it is what you call a coincidence. I saw the young man safely off, and he came up the other staircase. Madame can wear her white silk and lace, the diamonds will do with that—and look, the lovely roses Monsieur Vere send!" and she took from a side table a basket of sweet-scented tea roses, of rich warm colour.

"They *are* nice ; but, Cerise, isn't it a mercy the paste necklace came home in time," said Pauline, with nervous anxiety.

"Indeed, Madame, it is so ; but never mind about it. Madame has the necklace, and *the money !* That must always console Madame."

" Well, it does Cerise, certainly, but make haste and dress me. What a good thing I do not require any making up !"

" No ! " cried Cerise, affectionately. " Madame is *jeune et belle*, and if Madame would only not vex herself about so many small things, she will never be old ; her face is so *mignon*."

Cerise really loved her young mistress, indeed, she was as much a companion as attendant ; she was likewise perfectly aware of all the shortcomings of the master of the household ; but these she did not condemn.

All men were the same, *voila !* only it was
lâche of Monsieur to let her charming young
mistress be ever without money. Of course,
Madame resented that naturally.

Pauline looked very charming as she
passed down the softly-carpeted stairs, her
white   neck   and   arms   glistening   with
diamonds.   Her soft trailing dress of shim-
mering   silk,   with   its   lace   draperies,   her
brown   hair   piled   up   in   dainty   confusion
where   the   lovely   tea   roses   nestled,   as   also
in her dress.   Her cheeks were tinged with
the recent excitement.   Even her plethoric
husband, who had long since ceased to love
her, looked up with some show of awakened
interest, as she stepped daintily down the
broad stairs.

" I think those diamonds suit you, Mrs.
Cohen," said he. " That thousand wasn't
thrown away ; that necklace is worth every
penny of it ; it always represents money.

Mind you are careful of them; and you too,
Cerise."

" Certainly, Monsieur! "

Charlie Vere stood silently waiting,
holding Pauline's bouquet. He took the
wrap from Cerise, and carefully put it round
her. Then Mr. Cohen said: " Start on first
with Mrs. Cohen, I will join you in a very
few moments. I just want to call at the
club for something. I have a cab here, so
take the carriage. Pauline! what time is
Lady Carew's reception? "

" Ten. Are you going to that, as well as
the dinner at Lansdown Place? " asked his
wife, opening her black eyes in amazement.

" Yes. I have a particular reason for
going there. But don't delay; it is time
you were off."

Mrs. Cohen showed no particular curiosity
or interest in her husband's " reason."
" Shall we send the carriage to the club? "

Yes. He then put on his overcoat and passed out to his cab.

"Oh, Charlie, I have done such a stroke of business, but I have done it in fear and trembling."

"What is this wonderful 'stroke,' Mada-mina?"

"I have sold the diamond necklace and have got this paste one in its place. It looks exactly like the original," she added, with a nervous laugh.

"How *could* you be so imprudent?" he answered, his tone full of grave anxiety.

"It is all very well to say *imprudent*," she answered irritably. "But I simply can't and won't go on any longer without some proper supply of money that I can call my own. There is not a woman in London so abominably treated. Just as if I were a baby—and a married woman, too!"

"But, Pauline, it is your husband's property, I fear, you have been selling. Why did you not ask me? All I have is at your command. Nay, my life, if it would do you any good."

"Charlie, kind and good as you are, I could not take your money."

After a painful silence, he asked her to whom had she sold the jewels.

"To Storr and Lazenby's."

"How long ago?"

"About a week."

"Promise me that you will never do such a serious thing again without consulting me. I am sure it will lead to some terrible *esclandre*."

"Well, Charlie, I *will* promise, but I really can't see what there is to make all this terrible fuss about. They are my own, you know. Mr. Cohen gave them to me as a birthday present the first year of my marriage. I wanted some money. I sold them. *Voila tout!*"

" I hope it's not too late, that's all."

" Hope what is not ' too late'? You are getting enigmatical, Charlie."

" When did you send the necklace?"

" I *left* it, I told you, a week ago. I got the money for it to-night. There, that will do. You are nearly as disagreeable as Mr. Cohen," and she drew her wrap round her, and almost hid her face in its fleecy fur.

Charlie hardly heeded her petulance. He knew, which Mrs. Cohen did not, that her husband had been speculating heavily on the Stock Exchange, and, rumour had it, losing heavily. Hence he traced an under-current of purpose, in the choice by Mr. Cohen of his wife's jewels that night. And Charlie intended the first thing the next morning to go and get back the necklace at

any cost, before the dangerous transaction
came to the knowledge of Mr. Cohen.

Mr. Cohen did *not* arrive in time for the
dinner at Lansdown Place, though Pauline
wondered, and young Vere felt a secret
anxiety; but Mrs. Cohen would not allow
her hostess to delay her dinner, which
progressed gaily. Pauline was a great
favourite, and radiant!—her skeleton for
the nonce buried out of sight. She gave
out her brightness, as her bright eyes and
her jewels did their lustre.

The dinner was just over. The ladies
were about to withdraw from the men,
when a servant glided round to Mr. Vere,
and whispered in his ear. Pauline happened to catch the action, and saw a look
of anxiety pass over the young man's face.

"What is it?" she asked, authorita-
tively, of the man. "Is it from Mr.
Cohen?"

Mr. Cohen's coachman had brought word that his master had been taken ill with a fit at the club, and had been driven home at once. The news caused much sensation. Pauline, and Mr. Vere, left immediately, to find their home in a turmoil of excitement and anxiety, a doctor's carriage at the door. The servants thought it was an apoplectic fit or paralysis—they were not sure which — only he was insensible. Pauline hastily threw off her costly dress and her glittering gems, and, putting on a soft *robe-de-chambre*, hurried into her husband's chamber.

There lay the heavy, unconscious form of Mr. Cohen.

"What is it? Is it *very* serious?" she whispered, with white face, to the physician.

"I will tell you later on," he replied, with professional vagueness. " I am expecting Sir William Rowe. We will then give you our opinion, Mrs. Cohen."

"Is there *nothing* I can do?"

"Nothing. Reserve yourself," he said kindly, "in case you are wanted later on."

She passed out of the room. Mr. Vere was anxiously waiting on the landing.

"Oh, Charlie, he looks as white as death, and his face is drawn!"

"Come into your room; I want to ask you something."

"Don't ask me anything; I feel stupid and bewildered. Do as you like."

"Well, then, I have telegraphed for Lady Laura."

"For mamma! Whatever for? She cannot do any good, and, besides, *he* detests her."

"He need not see her. It is better for you, dear. Dear Pauline, *do* go and lie down for a little while. Your hands are burning, and you are feverish."

"How can you ask me to lie down? I have the doctors to see presently."

"Let me see them for you?"

"No, I will see them myself."

In truth Pauline was thoroughly frightened. It was her first experience of a great trouble, and, although there had been times when she had almost hated her husband, now that he was stricken down the better part of her nature asserted itself.

"I shall sit up all night with him; it is the least thing I can do."

He said no more. They both sat anxiously awaiting the doctor's verdict.

It seemed as if hours passed. Each silent—he, full of anxious forebodings; she, of nervous agitation. With him there was no thought of self, and for the young wayward wife of his guardian, such chivalrous love, and regard, as a brother might render in such an hour of need. Pauline was not given to much analysis of thought and feeling. There was a dumb consciousness of some impending catastrophe, an overshadowing of some unknown trial, and as she sat there, a face white and scared, he thought of the contrast of a few hours before.

By and-by Cerise came to tell them the doctors were in the dining-room, and would see Mrs. Cohen."

"Come, Charlie !"

They went down. Dr. Lechmere and Sir William Rowe came forward.

"Kindly tell me the exact truth."

"We fear there is no hope, Mrs. Cohen. There are complications beside the seizure. He may last till the morning," said Sir William kindly, seeing the white face of the young wife.

Dr. Lechmere drew young Vere aside.

" Can you not send for any female relation of Mrs. Cohen ? "

" I have telegraphed for her mother, Lady Laura Ridden. I know she will make every effort to be here to-night."

" That is well.   Mrs. Cohen is far too young to be left alone with such an anxious responsibility.   I will come in again presently.   I have procured a nurse who I know is already at her post, b ut nothing can be done, he will not rally."

" He was very good to me," said the young man, simply, and somehow the doctor liked him better for that little unconscious loyalty to the dying man.

Sir William Rowe left, and Pauline returned to her husband's room.   She saw the nurse at one side of the bed, but she hardly noticed her presence.

Her gaze was fixed on the large white

face, drawn to one side; the strongly
marked eyebrows, the closely-cut grey hair,
all stood out with solemn distinctness, while
the heavy breathing was all that spoke of
life in the heavy, inert body. Then their
brief, but ill-starred married life, the in-
fidelity of her husband, her own shortcomings, her wayward coldness and ill-
concealed dislike. She judged herself
very severely during this solemn vigil; face
to face with herself, she seemed to see a
light, frivolous, empty creature. The night
passed into the still grey morning. Lady
Laura had arrived, but her daughter did
not go to greet her. She knew kind faithful Charlie would do that. Cerise brought
her in a cup of coffee, which she insisted
upon her mistress drinking. As the day
dawned she fancied he moved. She leant
over him, and took the nerveless hand.
Oh, Louis! if you could only make one

sign. She stooped over and kissed the pale, calm forehead, it seemed cold and severe. Ah, it was many a long day since she had kissed him. The fact came home with some remorse. The doctor had been in and out noiselessly, several times during the night, but this time he gently raised the blind, and the cold grey of the new-born day lighted the room with sad quiet light. He looked at the bed, and the light settled on a grey reflection.

"Let me lead you to your room, Mrs. Cohen," said the doctor, with firm kindness.

"Certainly not! As long as my husband lives, my place is here."

"He is not here," he said gently.

"Oh! Doctor Lechmere, are you quite, quite sure?"

Presently young Vere came in, and gently moved the quiet cold hand.

After a while, she consented to leave the
room, and Charlie led her to her own
sitting-room, where her mother anxiously
awaited her. She folded her in her arms
with affectionate love, and all she said was
"Rest yourself, dear, your work is over."

Cerise then brought her mistress a glass
of wine, for she was chilled by her long
watch, and her nerves were over-wrought.

"Go to rest, madame."

"What o'clock is it, mother?"

"Six, dearest!"

"Will Madame please go to bed?" said
Cerise, with quiet presistency.

"Yes, I suppose so," answered Pauline,
wearily.

"Have you attended to my mother?"

"Indeed, she has, and so has Mr. Vere."

Yes, Lady Louisa had to admit Charlie
Vere was a most useful person. He it was,
in all the confusion thought of *her*, the

tired, weary, anxious traveller, told Cerise
to bring up a dainty little supper, and saw
to her every comfort.

"Where is poor Charlie, mother?"

"In the dining-room, in case you require
him."

"Cerise, tell him to go to bed."

"Certainly! When Madame is in bed."

"How you bother, Cerise," said Pauline,
irritably.

"*Mais oui!* It is time for Madame to be
in bed, and Miladi also."

"Go! Mamma, dear. You look fagged
out."

"Very well; we will both go."

Cerise would not leave Mrs. Cohen until
she was safely in bed, where very soon a
heavy sleep overtook her—and at last, all
the household were at rest.

CHAPTER X.

WHEN Lady Laura Ridden lay down to
rest, that daybreak so full of solemn events,
her first feeling was one of thankfulness!
Thankfulness that the death of her son-in-
law had removed the greatest of anxieties,
and dissolved in a dignified manner a union
that promised to become a punishment to
both parties. Mr. Cohen, in Lady Laura's
opinion, had atoned for much, nay, for
everything, by dying just when he did. It
was the one clear way out of many bristling
difficulties. Yes; she was thankful; for
in her way, she did love her child dearly,
and that child had been on the brink of
an abyss, and by this unlooked-for release
she had been saved. In the privacy of her
own chamber Lady Laura planned many

things for the future, but unfortunately for her calculation her daughter was an " unknown quantity." The mother might build and scheme, but Mrs. Cohen had a way of doing exactly the opposite of what was expected of her, and Lady Laura could not let events settle themselves—which they often do ; much better, in the long run, than anything she might have arranged.

After the funeral, when the will was read, instead of Mr. Cohen being the wealthy millionaire, it was generally supposed, it was discovered, that, owing to unlucky speculations, and the unexpected failure of a great American firm, in which he was greatly involved, the once princely fortune was reduced to a few thousands. However, with the sale of the lavishly furnished house and her marriage settlement, Pauline would find herself the possessor of no mean income ; and, so far as she was

concerned, there was no acute sorrow.
She had never professed to love her husband; nay, it must be confessed there was
a sense of liberty at the bottom of everything. She would be mistress of an income
which seemed, in her inexperienced eyes, a
small fortune. She would have no trouble
whatever. Charlie was one of the trustees;
he would take care she was not bothered.

So she settled to go on the Continent.

It was a dull November evening when
Charlie saw the two ladies off—gloomy and
foggy, but it did not seem to affect
Pauline; on the contrary, her pretty piquant
face looked charming under her widow's
weeds. It was in vain Lady Laura behaved
herself with extra regard to the most
thorough conventional proprieties; there
was a mutinous wilfulness about her
daughter that was not to be suppressed,
and she only looked what she felt. No

prisoner could be expected to envelope himself in sackcloth and ashes if the governor of his prison happened to expire. All the more if the prisoner's time of service was up, and he started again with the blessed privileges of freedom. And for the first time in her life Pauline felt free, and she meant to realise this freedom. She was amply supplied with money. This pleasant change of their lives, was to be no expense to her mother, and this thought alone was pleasant. The poor dear mother who had been struggling and striving bravely for years, should now have a fine time, without having to suffer for it afterwards.

"Don't be long before you join us, Charlie," said Pauline just as the train was steaming out of the station. "We shall want you in Paris; I mean to see a lot!"

"I will, Mrs. Cohen! But you see the

other trustee can't get along without me just at present; I shall be over soon, though, as I shall want your signature to some papers."

"The sooner the better, Charlie."

Lady Laura could not help giving expression to her vexation, at always having young Vere tacked on to them. Was this young man for ever to be an appanage of her daughter's establishment."

"Cannot you really do without Mr. Vere for even two or three months?" said Lady Laura when they were once on their way.

"No, I really cannot, mamma!" said Pauline with pleasant alacrity. "I have been so used to him nearly every day for five years, so of course I can't do without him. He is mixed up with everything. I could as soon do without Cerise—by-the-bye, I wonder if she is quite handy in the next carriage? It is a second class, isn't it mother?" And Mrs. Cohen, without wait-

ing for her mother's answer, put her head
out of her own window. " Well, I really
can't see at the rate we are going at, so it is
no good speculating ! "

" Pauline ! " said her mother, bringing
back the conversation, she had interrupted
in her own irrelevant fashion, to the point.
" You must remember you are a young
widow, good-looking,' passably rich. It
really does not look *comme il faut* to see that
young fellow always dangling about you."

" For the matter of that he won't be
always dangling after me, because I shall
probably marry him, he suits me so well,"
said Mrs. Cohen composedly.

" Perhaps he may not wish to marry
you," said her mother drily.

" Oh, there is no fear of that ! " said
Pauline with airy confidence.

" Pauline, do you remember Gerald
Lanyon ? "

" Perfectly ! "

" Would you like to see him again ? "

" I don't mind one way or the other," said the younger woman with honest indifference. " He is a parson now—I don't like parsons."

" I hear nothing but good of him."

" That is just it ! He would be much too good, and bore me frightfully. Charlie never bores me. On the contrary, when I feel a fit of what our ancestors called 'the vapours,' he always acts as a stimulant and does me good."

Pauline saw through her mother's lightly veiled diplomacy, but she meant to enjoy her future life in her own way, and that way included Mr. Vere's companionship. As far as her volatile nature allowed, she had loved Gerald Lanyon, but that was so long ago ; it was all dead and buried, and the grass growing greenly over that grave.

"Mother! do you know Charlie and I have settled and rearranged your money affairs! When you have your bank book made up next time you will find a snug little balance to the good, and you can snap your fingers at that disagreeable old aunt Caroline and the Framptons generally."

"Pauline!"

"It is a fact, dear! It was no use saying one word until it was done. Do you think I am going to enjoy all sorts of luxuries while you are striving and pinching, and accepting doles from those nasty stuck-up Framptons! Stingy old things! My lord can keep his money."

"Oh, Pauline, how can I accept such a thing—your money, too!"

"That's just it, Mamsy. It is because it is mine! Wouldn't you? Nay! you did your very best for me years ago, trying to turn me out well, and often going without things essential to your position ; and now —we need not say a word about it again— it's a *fait accompli*."

The tears stood in Lady Laura's eyes. She had not given her daughter credit for so much affection or thought, and she felt deeply touched. Pauline kissed her mother, and it was the dawn of happier times to them both.

CHAPTER XI.

LADY LOUISA and Gerald Lanyon paid their promised visit to the Towers, and if Gerald had been so agreeably disappointed at finding an intelligent, cultivated woman, in the person of Miss Higgins, he was still more surprised when he saw her in her own home—the house with its many charming details, its grounds, its refined interior. No wonder time flew! And so it came to pass, that instead of the junior curate foreswearing the company of all feminines, as was his wont, he was loth to leave when the time came to say good-bye, but Lady Louisa was peremptory, and dragged him away.

" My dear Gerald, you can come again you know. The Rector will rebel if I am too long away."

"To be sure. How selfish I am."

"Not a bit! it is enchanted ground. I always find great difficulty in getting away. It is such a restful place, Gerald; there is such a quiet, calm dignity about it all. I think Hester is such a very charming woman, and really not at all plain, as some people say."

"Plain!" said Gerald, warmly. "Far from that. There is something so womanly and good about her, and so generous. There are some natures so meanly dowered, that if they were asked for five pounds out of their store of plenty, they would deny the gift or loan."

"I think that is by no means an uncommon phase of character, especially in people blessed with wealth. They are so afraid of reducing their store by driblets, often forgetting the large sums they will spend upon some hobby,

11*

which is entirely for their own gratification."

"Miss Higgins is a wise steward, and deserves happiness," said Mr. Lanyon.

"I hope, with all my heart," said her ladyship, affectionately, "she will marry some day, and find a husband worthy of her. Gerald! did you hear of the sad death of Mr. Cohen?"

"Yes; Lady Laura wrote and told me."

"Lady Laura! and when?"

"About three weeks ago."

Lady Louisa was silent a few moments. She was mentally reviewing the situation; but she thought she had checkmated her sister, none too soon though.

"It was a sad termination to such an ambitious marriage," said Gerald Lanyon presently, but Lady Louisa observed he said it with quiet indifference; and he almost felt surprised himself, at the absence

of all disturbance, which, a few months
back, would have certainly followed the
details of this strange and sudden collapse
of Lady Laura Ridden's plans. He felt
interested in another woman. Yes, he
admitted so much; but most certainly he
was not in love with her. Oh, no! he felt
convinced, although he no longer felt the
very faintest trace of love for his once
idolised Pauline, he certainly had no idea
of loving anyone else. But it was a very
pleasant thing in life to meet with a good
woman, and one who was his equal
mentally, perhaps his superior. He did
feel grateful to his old friend, Lady Louisa,
for after all, he argued, a man does require,
as a stimulant, the society of an intelligent
agreeable woman.

" *Il est doux de voir ses amis par goût et
par estime; il est pénible de les cultiver par
intérêt, c'est solliciter.*"

Yes, it was from taste and esteem, that her society gave him pleasure, and from no other motive.

Two or three months had passed, the quaint old gardens in the town had donned their autumn garb, the holyoaks had given place to the chrysanthemums, the leaves from the old trees were softly falling in golden showers, but life went quietly on with each change. Miss Higgins and Esmé were still at the Towers. She had discovered a fresh interest in life. And Gerald Lanyon was now a constant visitor. He was no longer a curate, to be kept at a distance, but a true and valued friend—a man who found life a very earnest thing, who, after a sharp struggle with sorrow, found his eyes cleared, and was able to measure the distance he hoped to travel without any deceitful mirage to distract him, whose self-reliant strength, was a source of comfort to those who relied upon him.

His patients and friends at Combe Warren had left their encampment, taking with them many substantial tokens of his kindness. A large fire of gorse and under-wood signalised their departure. The temporary hospital had been cleared away, and nothing but the blackened space showed where the wandering people had lived and suffered. Even their old cara-vans had been burned, and new ones built at their generous friend's expense.

Mr. Dashwood was still the model curate at St. Just, leaving nothing undone that could be done effectively and well. Never were the services so well appointed as when Mr. Dashwood was in command. He was still as indefatigable as ever in his siege to Combe Towers, but the chariot-wheels of this portion of his work dragged heavily,

and he fancied Esmé's eyes were not as
friendly as of yore. But he persevered;
the end would crown the work!

Whatever Percy Blythe did had a very
honest ring about it; but he was apt to be
forgetful—Cyril Dashwood never forgot!
But if the Rector had been asked in confidence which of his curates he preferred,
he would undoubtedly have answered,
"Blythe." When the little vexations, and
sometimes the big ones, bothered him more
than usual, it was to Percy he would come
for help or sympathy. Blythe was the
one to smooth over the little difficulties, or
to suggest a pleasant *Deus ex Machinâ* out
of the big ones. There was something so
human in him and so indulgent towards all
creation generally. But there was one thing
few knew about, or how much self-denial it
involved, how often it compelled him to
wear his clothes till they almost remon-

strated with their owner by their shining seams, but little extra comforts found their way to the beloved and widowed mother, and the little delicate sister. These little transactions were in strict confidence with himself.

Mrs. Frostick was as busy as ever with her own and other people's affairs, the Miss Brown's especially; also Mrs. Grantley came in for her share of notice from the town gossip, but in this case she counted without her host.

At one of the tea-drinking afternoons, so dear to the elderly female heart, Mrs. Frostick, with many mysterious winks and nods, had given out in solemn tones the forthcoming marriage of Mrs. Grantley and Mr. Blythe! Dearie me! Laws now! You don't say so! and such like, fell from many lips—all eager to be the first to impart the wonderful news elsewhere; it rolled like a snowball, gathering force and volume as it flew onwards, till at last it reached the Rector's ears.

"I say, *Lewis*, is it *true* your sister, Mrs. Grantley, is about to marry my curate, Blythe? Everyone has it so!"

"My sister Edith marry young Blythe! Preposterous! My dear Rector, where did you get *that* from? Ha! ha! it is really too absurd."

"Well, I was rather surprised myself!"

"Oh, I must tell Edith that! What a strange place a country town is for 'canards.'"

But Edith took the matter very calmly. "I know where *that* comes from! from Mrs. Bostick! I don't mind betting five pounds! The old cat! Can't you go and frighten her Edward? It would be a charity all round, and pay off lots of old scores for other people."

"But are we quite sure dear, it *is* her?"

"My dear Edward, I am positive! Ah, it's the 'Wig' asserting itself!"

"The what? My dear Edith!"

"Oh, never mind, Edward, get yourself up, and take the carriage and pair, the two men servants, and just drive down in style to the old witch's house! Ask to see her in the most amiable manner, and *then* let fly the vials of your wrath. Excuse the expression, it is not elegant, but it conveys my feelings."

Dr. Lewis shook his head. "I don't care for the errand, Edie."

"My dear Edward, it is so simple! Express your severe disapprobation at her presuming, &c., &c., to discuss my affairs."

The Mayor set out on his mission, and when the well-appointed carriage drew up abruptly at Mrs. Frostick's door, that lady was in a flutter of excitement. "Betty, surely they are going to invite me to some

grand gala! Ask the Mayor into the best
front parlour." The Mayor did not sit
down as requested, but began at once.

"Mrs. Frostick! by what authority did
you spread the report of Mrs. Grantley's
engagement to one of the young curates?"

"I heard it reported."

"By whom? I shall be obliged by the
author's name." Mrs. Frostick shuffled her
feet, and twisted her thumbs, but no help
came; there stood the Mayor, glaring at
her through his spectacles.

"If you cannot produce your authority,
there is only one conclusion to come to, that
you and *you* alone spread these reports con-
cerning my sister. And, therefore, you will
be so good as to contradict them *at once*,
and by the same means that you spread
them. Good morning!" and he marched
off to his carriage, without another word.
"Lack-a-day! Well, to be sure!"

"Well, mistress, and what did his worship say? Is it a dinner, or a party?" cried Betty, rushing in.

"Hold your tongue, and wait till you're spoken to," replied her mistress angrily.

"Lord save us!" and then Betty wisely concluded the Mayor's visit could not have been so very pleasant, for her mistress's 'front' was viciously pulled over her forehead, and her cap pushed back. To say that she was angry and mortified, was only a portion of the truth. She felt sure she would not be asked to the first winter reception, which would be coming off within three weeks, and it meant a public humiliation to her, not to be seen with all the others. Her *prestige* as an important person would be gone. She had been weighed in the balance against Mrs. Grantley, and found herself considerably wanting.

While she was in this unenviable frame
of mind, one of her principal cronies, seeing
the Mayor's carriage had just started on its
return journey, rushed in to hear the
wonderful news.

" What did the Mayor want of you, Mrs.
Frostick?   It must have been something
particular.   He never brings you carriage
unless it's something important. What is it,
neighbour ? "

" Only some private affair the Mayor had
to tell me.   Oh, I find Mrs. Grantley isn't
to marry yon curate after all ? "

" Isn't to marry him !   Why they say the
wedding was to be next month, and I do
hear the presents are something wonderful!
It's too bad folks changing their minds like
that !   Who's to know what's what ? "

To all this Mrs. Frostick said nothing.
She knew the 'town' would consider itself
defrauded, and she had been responsible.

However, she meant to show a bold front.

"Well, Mrs. Hughes, I am real busy to-day. We are just cleaning up for Christmas."

"Aye, to be sure! ours is just over." And Mrs. Hughes, seeing a fellow housekeeper with all the severe solemnity of May-Day and Martinmas heavy on her conscience, appreciated the gravity of the situation, and considerately departed.

In a fortnight's time came Mrs. Frostick's punishment. The Brown girls had got cards for the Mayor and Mayoress's reception, November the ninth. This was the first and most exclusive of these receptions. There was nothing for it. She *must* be *ill!* She chose to have an attack of 'Tic,' it was safe, and she need not have a doctor! Betty could not understand it at all, and her brains not being of the first order, quietly gave it up, only giving her version of the affair. "The Mayor had indeed, called to see *her* mistress, to invite her to a grand dinner; but the mistress was a bit ailing, and so couldn't go." Mrs. Frostick certainly owed a debt of gratitude to her faithful Betty, for there was no doubt now, she had quarrelled with the powers that be, and had got the worst of it.

"And so you have been asked to dinner with the Mayor, Mrs. Frostick?" said old David Brown to his old neighbour.

"How folks do talk!" answered she, evasively.

"Aye! they do. They've nought else to do. It's surprising what time idle folks has for mischief. How is your 'Tic' to-day, ma'am?"

"Better, thank you, Mr Brown!"

The town has been real busy to-day. Dr. Lewis again Mayor—Aye, he's a good one. You see, neighbour, when they choose a tradesman, it takes a lot of their time up, whereas Dr. Lewis, being a gentleman with money, as you may say, and having nothing else to do but catch beetles, flies, and other vermin, and go about with them archæologists, and——"

"Eh! David Brown, what *are* they folk?"

"Well," said he, scratching his head, not too sure of his own knowledge. "I *think* they be people who go hunting up old tombs, and burial grounds, and churches, and old buildings—people with naught else but 'fads'—I take it."

"Aye," and she sniffed contemptuously, "likely enough."

"They do say," continued old Brown, "he's mighty clever, and for certain, he's real good and kind. Bless you! you should see how good he's been to that family down by the river, them that had the ague. He's doctored them, fed them, and sent them down to the sea ! And Mrs. Grantley too—she is a real lady to be sure! she's mighty kind to my lassies. Says she, 'Tell them to come up and have tea with me, Mr. Brown.' She's smart, and clever, no mistake, and as bonnie as she's high. I can't say I'm a bit sorry she isn't going to marry Parson Blythe ; not that I've a *word* to say agin him, he's as nice and kind a young fellow as ever walked, but he ain't to my mind, good enough for her. Now, Mr. Lanyon is more proud like, and he will be a great man, I'm told. Now, if it was *he !* He's older and richer, and, they do say, knows a thing or two."

"She'll have none of him, you may be sure," snapped Mrs. Frostick. "He isn't too keen on any woman, he can't abide 'em."

"Well, neighbour Frostick, they all know their own affairs best—what they like, and what they don't—and I must say you might have a worse lot. From the Rector, and Lady Louisa, bless her! downwards, they are as nice and kind a set as I have ever come across—all real good gentlefolks."

"I don't complain of them, do I?"

"Nay, nay, to be sure not! Good-day, neighbour, good-day!" And old Brown went out, with the conviction that his old neighbour was, "uncommon snappish; but folks is most cross when they are ill, and, perhaps, she's lonesome like, and she's no bairns." Kind old man, who saw so few faults in his own children; to him they were always the "Bairns," and any little kindness shown to them always won his heart. That there was anything foolish or ridiculous about them, never

12*

entered *his* simple old head, and even Mrs. Frostick was forbearing with him on this point. They administered to all his wants, kept his house spotlessly clean—what more could a man expect from any woman? *His* little amusements could be so cheaply and happily had at the " Queen's Head " ; and his daughters could take theirs in their own way.

CHAPTER XII.

One fine afternoon, towards the end of November, one of those exhilarating days that do sometimes shine out as golden in that usually dreary month, when the sense of living is a pleasure—the crisp frosty air tinctured with the aroma from the trees. The sun brilliant and clear, the sky an exquisite blue, with just a few fleecy clouds flitting along in airy pursuit of each other. The few yet unfallen leaves, still golden, still red, clinging to their bare branches, as if loth to leave, and sigh out their own knell as they flutter to earth, to be absorbed like the thousands before them.

On such a day Gerald Lanyon walked over to Combe Towers. He could not

have told you why he felt such an elasti-
city, such a gaiety of heart, such a sense of
brightness within and without. He walked
with light, brisk step till he came near to
the house, and then he felt a sudden access
of shyness. He had come on an errand on
which hung his whole life. At last he
realised that he was no longer heart free.
The love of his youth had faded away like
a beautiful dreamy mist that eludes the
touch and the thoughts. But this love of
his manhood was grand, real—a power to
his whole being. How would it be with
him this day? He reached the gate, and
Hester was just coming through with her
dog.

"Whither away?"

"Only for a walk through the plantation. The scent of the trees is so delicious.
It reminds me of the pine forests abroad."

"May I come with you? I have something to ask you, some great favour at your hands."

" Nay! you have only to command ; you know that."

"Is it so, I wonder?" he answered, looking at her keenly. " Come, let us go on, then !

" Miss Higgins, some years ago there was a young fellow without fame, without fortune. Perhaps I may say his birth was good, but that was an accident. He had been associated day by day, year by year (for they both lived in the same village), in intimate friendship with a family that was very dear to him. A fair young girl grew up with him, and became as the apple of his eye. All his future was bounded by her, all his present tinged by her. She was fresh and dainty as a young rose. At length he ventured to lay his hopes before her mother. I will briefly

add his dreams were brutally crushed.
The mother coldly told him she had other
views for her daughter. They henceforth
passed out of his life, leaving him ship-
wrecked, starving for one drop of consola-
tion. The girl afterwards married a rich
man twice her age. They can be dismissed. An illness to the man followed.
He became hard, cynical, almost unendur-
able. A friend, who had been his tutor, at
last roused him to nobler things than the
miserable study of his disappointments.
He became a worker for a Master who
deals more mercifully than man, and at
last he found peace. After some few years
another woman came across his path, a
woman nobly planned, born to comfort
and command. Once more his heart has
gone forth with a stronger grasp. For on
this woman depends his happiness; in her
hand lies his fate ! ''

He turned abruptly round, his face working with strong emotion. " Hester, what is to be your answer ? "

Her eyes were full of tender tears. She placed both her hands in his.

" If I am worthy of this honour, then indeed I am yours."

He needed no more, but clasped her in his arms. And then, as he looked into her face, there came into it a new and beautiful light, such as Esmé had partially seen. As if Hester's world had suddenly become radiant, the possibilities so longed after had become absolute realities! Heart to heart, soul to soul—both had been tried in the fire. Hester's inner beauty had been hidden from the world. To them her face had been dull and cold and severe. Now—now the grey eyes had a depth, and the cheeks a lovely flush—love had beautified it, and henceforth took possession !

"Hester! what a beautiful face is yours!"

"Ah, no! Your love makes you blind."

"On the contrary, it has opened my eyes! It is a good thing to have that love that casteth out fear and is clothed with mutual trust. Ah, love! love, I have been so fearful!"

"Of what?" said she with beaming eyes.

"Can you not guess? Suppose you had said 'No'!"

"Did it dawn upon you that I might love, too?—though there is so little about me to attract," she said with great humility.

"Hester, I will not allow you to depreciate yourself," said he with loving authority, taking her hand and putting it through his arm. "You cannot know what I think of you, my queen; but, please God, my life shall show."

They wandered on, they hardly realized the afternoon had deepened into twilight, that evening was just upon them, that the stars were coming out one by one. Old Major, soberly walking beside Hester, every now and again, rubbed his cold soft nose against her hand. No, she never heeded him, though she realized he was there. It seemed as if this hour of glorious happiness atoned for her long life of heart hunger. It required the deep clang of the dressing bell from Combe Towers, which pealed forth protestingly to its absent mistress, to bring them back to earth.

"Oh, how late it is! It is the first bell. Gerald, you will come in and dine with us? Ah, do!" And she laid her hand entreatingly on his arm as he shook his head.

"No! sweetheart! I *must* be back—and in haste too; but I shall go on wings. I have so much to make up—I mean such arrears of happiness. I shall see you safely to your door. Kiss me once more, love!

We shall speedily meet again." And so they parted at the outer gate.

"Hester! Hester! We were getting quite anxious about you," cried Esmé, as she flew down the broad stairs, her soft white draperies floating behind her.

"Where *have* you been, dear? The first bell was rung some time ago! Why, what a lovely colour you have! but your eyelashes are wet, dear!"

For the lamp, so daintily held, on the first landing, by a graceful bronze figure of an Egyptian maiden, threw its full, soft light on the tear-stained but happy face of Hester.

"It is the dew, love! or perhaps a *soupçon* of frost!" she answered with a gay smile.

"Mrs. Grantley, Mr. Blythe, and Sir Ernest Beldon have just come, but the D octor hasn't turned up yet."

"I won't be five minutes, Esmé, send Justine to my room at once. And then go into the drawing-room, and entertain our guests, until I come."

"Justine is already in your room, dear!"

And there Hester found her, amazed, but too discreet to make any observation at the unusual absence of her mistress. "I have put out Mademoiselle's black lace with crimson!"

"That will do, Justine, only be as quick as you can, I am late."

Justine's busy fingers rapidly completed the change in her mistress's toilet.

A very short time elapsed, and Hester joined her guests; she looked stately and handsome, as she made her apologies.

Mrs. Grantley instantly noticed the soft colour still visible, and the unwonted light in the grey eyes.

"There's a man in the case! I am sure! Now who can it be?" thought the little lady sagaciously.

Lady Louisa, with all discreetness, had held her peace. No one in fact knew anything of the intimacy between Gerald Lanyon and the inmates of "Combe Towers." He would be the last person suspected of even the faintest *tendresse* for any woman.

"I don't see the Doctor!" said Hester.

"I expect him every moment! some of his especial patients," said his step-sister with a laugh, "sent for him just as we were about to start, so Mr. Blythe escorted me instead, and my brother will ride."

"The dinner bell has not rung yet, so he will be in good time after all," said Miss Higgins.

And as she spoke, Dr. Lewis was announced.

"How bright and cheery the room

looks, Miss Higgins! One may say, with fair Portia :

'The light we see, is burning in my Hall,
How far that little candle throws his beams.'

I quite pitied the man whom I met coming *from*, instead of coming *to it!*"

"Who was he?" asked Mrs. Grantley, promptly.

"Gerald Lanyon!"

"So! *that's* it," thought she, and a little amused smile flitted over her face.

"Why, Lanyon has a meeting on at his house to-night! about his hospital; a lot of big-wigs are to be there," said Mr. Blythe.

"Well! I suppose he was hurrying to it, for he seemed to be walking with seven-leagued boots! He hardly spoke to me, he was in such haste"

To Hester's great thankfulness, the

butler announced the dinner, and so saved
her further embarrassment.

     *   *   *   *   *

Never, in all the years of her life, had
Hester tasted such exquisite happiness as
she felt this night. She longed for the
solitude of her own chamber, that she
might at length realise it. As it was,
there was an infectious brightness about
her. She seemed to convey some of the
gladsomeness of her own heart to her
guests. There was some subtle influence
about her, that they could not analyze,
only it affected them.

She felt greatly pleased to see the
little merry interchange of *badinage* between Sir Ernest and Esmé. Esmé had by
no means given up her love for handsome
Cyril Dashwood, but it was gradually, and
surely wearing itself out. And Hester left
affairs to arrange themselves; but she saw

with thankfulness that the cloud on the soft young face was gently dispersing, and sunshine taking its place.

Just as the guests were departing, Sir Ernest came up ·quietly to Hester, and whispered—"Do you think I *ever* shall succeed with her?"

And with a smile, Hester answered him:

> "Hope is a lover's staff, walk hence with that,
> And manage it against despairing thoughts."

"Good-night, dear friend, and take that for your comfort. It is good advice."

"I will," said he, hopeful at once.

When Hester retired to her own chamber that night, she seemed to feel, nay, to look younger! Happiness, and love, are the most perfect cosmetics that have ever been fashioned in this world—nothing less than a divine spark from above. And it was herself! not her wealth! that was the joy with her. She felt *thankful* that the man she loved had, and would have, ample means. In this alone, Fortune had been good to her, for if her lover had been poor, then her own wealth would have been a frightful barrier, for Mr. Lanyon would have been far too proud to have married any woman dowered with such wealth as hers. But he was her equal, nay, in her humbleness, she said her superior.

"And to think what we shall have—and to spare—for those that need! If I have waited long for it, Happiness has come at last! Ah, if he *had* not loved me! what should I have become; because I love him so well! Now there are two of us, but united—

"'All who joy would win
Must share it—happiness was born a twin.'"

As yet, Hester did not tell Esmé, her

dear old friend the Rector's wife must be the first to hear this great news; but it was too new as yet—too sacred—it was her own to think over, and to cherish; and with this last feeling of thankfulness, she closed her eyes.

CHAPTER XIII.

AFTER his meeting was over, Gerald Lanyon walked over to the Rectory. He felt, in spite of the general reserve of his nature, that he *must* have the sympathy of Lady Louisa and the joy of telling her his beautiful news. He found his old friend somewhat excited; an open letter lay before her.

"Oh, Gerald! there you are, just as I wanted you. My sister Laura and her daughter are anxious to come down here for a month, before they settle in town for the winter, for it appears Lady Laura's brother-in-law has died rather suddenly, but I am thankful to say has left her a nice little fortune, which, later on, will come to Pauline. I am *so* thankful—about the money I mean! it has been such a sad thing for Laura to be always cramped for means—it will so soften her, poor dear!"

"I am *very* glad for her sake," said he, kindly.

"But now, Gerald, where can I find rooms for them, with the servants they will bring?"

"Wait a little! I think I can manage it. First, I have two distinct items of news to tell you. My dearest friend! Hester has promised to be my wife."

"Gerald! I *am* thankful. She is the best and truest woman I know. You are made for each other! God bless you *both*, my dears." And she drew down his face to her own level and affectionately kissed him. "I will go over to-morrow and see her."

"Ah, do! dear godmother! Now for my second item. I heard this evening, from my

uncle's confidential servant, that Sir Horace
has had a fresh attack of illness, which has
weakened him very seriously, and he is very
anxious I should go and see him, and stay
some little time. So, if the Rector will
kindly spare me, I shall set off to-morrow,
and Lady Laura can have the entire use of
my cottage, with Mrs. Bayliss in command.
You know, Lady Louisa, it is the first time
since my poor cousin's death, that my uncle
has even expressed a wish to see me. I
expect he feels lonely, poor old man. I
will send most of my especial treasures
over to you, or to Hester, and then the
cottage can soon be made shipshape for
your sister and niece, and *should* I require
a shakedown here, I shall come to you, of
course."

"Your arrangement will do admi-
rably, Gerald. I quite begin to see my
way."

"Very well. Till to-morrow, then, good night. I am going home to smoke the pipe of peace, and think over my new-found happiness."

"My dear Laura," thought Lady Louisa, as the door closed on Gerald, "you are too late. The bird is flown, and the nest empty. Fancy my outwitting Laura!" said she, aloud.

"What is that about Laura?" said the Rector, coming in.

"Nothing; only she wants a house here until Christopher Ridden's affairs are settled."

Then she told him about Gerald, of his uncle's illness, and of his offer of the cottage, but nothing as yet of Hester.

"I expect Sir Horace Lanyon will wish his nephew to stay with him for good. It is only natural. He is an old man, and not likely to live long."

" But we shall miss Gerald, and, to put it mildly, my dear, his money. He has been *most* generous with it, and saved the funds a great deal. And about the Cottage Hospital? It is a great responsibility. He has undertaken so much—he and Miss Higgins together, I mean—as regards the money."

" Harry, they will be sure and see it well through. I know them both too well for that doubt ever to trouble me."

" Well, my dear, you always were romantic, but I trust in this case your clear common sense will rule this prognostication."

" I am *sure* of it."

" Very well, love. When does Lanyon wish to go ? "

" To-morrow."

"Of course he must," said the Rector, with a regretful sigh. " But just think,

Louisa, of losing a curate with eight hundred a year, who draws no salary, and works as hard as if he were paid for it."

"But you could not expect to keep him for ever, Harry. Why, he may be a bishop some day. It is quite on the cards. They always do, you know, choose men of position and means."

There was no gainsaying anything Lady Louisa had put forth. So the Rector resigned himself to what he could not possibly alter.

The next morning, Lady Louisa and Gerald drove over to the Towers. It was early morning, and the crisp frosty air was as yet untouched by the sun. Hester was surprised, but full of interest about Gerald's intended visit to Luscombe Manor. It was a fresh page in her new life. Then he told her about the expected inmates of his cottage.

"Oh, Gerald, it is your old love!" and a quick blush swept over her face.

"Yes, but not my new love, or my *true* love. Will you not trust me, Hester?"

'Oh, yes! pray forgive me."

Lady Louisa stood by, but they took little heed of her, beyond including her in everything that concerned themselves.

"My dear, I can answer for his love for you. Did I not hear his confession last night? Pauline Cohen is an unknown personage, added to which that young lady has bestowed herself on young Vere, and is only waiting just a year of decency to marry him, much to my sister's vexation, I must say," said her ladyship, with a little laugh.

"Dearest Hester," whispered he, "our time is brief, come into the conservatory, for a few last words." Esmé discreetly carried off Lady Louisa to show her a new

list of promised snbscribers to the forthcoming cottage hospital.

"Hester thinks of taking a house for
six weeks or two months in London, Lady
Louisa."

"Well, dear, and a very nice plan too."

"Rubinstein and some other great people
are going to have some chamber concerts.
You know we are both rather crazed on
music, and do mean to enjoy it. I am long-
ing for it."

This plan had been mooted, and
suggested, before Gerald Lanyon and
Hester Higgins had made the great plan
of their lives; also Hester was actuated by
another motive. She fancied if she with-
drew Esmé from the somewhat dangerous
proximity of Mr. Dashwood's neighbourhood, and gave Sir Ernest Beldon a
standing invite to their house in town, it
might bring matters to a climax.

Little Esmé's eyes were sharp, if soft and pretty. She had her own ideas as to Hester's secret regard for the ugly curate, and she watched it maturing with affectionate interest, but like the wise little woman she was, like the discreet statue, she saw everything and said nothing, but she did not know as yet that her friend's affairs were settled.

The conference over in the conservatory, Mr. Lanyon and Miss Higgins returned, both looking so beaming and radiant, that they could each say :—

"My love doth so approve him,
   That even his stubbornness, his checks and frowns,
Have grace and favour in them."

And certainly Mr. Lanyon left with his heart, and face too, full of grace and favour.

That evening, when the household had retired, Hester softly entered Esmé's room.

The young girl was lying in her cosy nest, but wide awake, cogitating over her own affairs. The elder woman came, and sat at the foot of the bed.

"Esmé, my Pygmalion has arrived at last! and your Hester has entered her new life. Does it surprise you, love?"

"No, darling Hester, it does not surprise me! but it pleases me greatly. I knew," she said, clapping her hands with triumph, "what it was coming to. My dear! you and Mr. Lanyon look a great deal too happy to deceive *anybody!* your humble servant included. Well, dear old Hester, you will have your staff to lean on"

"Yes, but to make my happiness perfect, some other dear little personage must have a staff as well. Think over it, darling, and God bless you."

Lady Louisa was very happy; she was

charmed with her own skilful generalship, that had brought about such a desirable climax! And the delightful part of it was, that no one knew anything about it (except perhaps little Esmé Curtis). She quite enjoyed this little mystery. When it was common property, the edge would be taken off, but as yet it was all her own.

But sooner than she imagined, she was to have a diplomatic victory.

About a week after Gerald Lanyon's departure, Lady Laura came down as a sort of *avant courier*, for the joint company of herself, daughter, and as many servants as the cottage would hold.

The two sisters were comfortably sitting over their afternoon tea, in the pretty Rectory drawing-room. A log of wood was hissing and crackling with pleasant vehemence in the old-fashioned grate, in spite of the winter sun, shining with feeble, though genial effulgence into the room, lighting it up with gentle rays. Lady Louisa was occupied, as usual, with her knitting, her pretty white plump hands moving as swiftly as her thoughts.

Lady Laura altogether looked more prosperous, and happier, than she had done for many a long day—she looked hopeful! Her sister's cheerful and homely countenance, bore a look of subdued excitement, which rather puzzled the elder lady.

"How very nice of Gerald Lanyon to lend us his cottage! I hope we shall not put him about much!"

"Oh no! I am sure you will not. In fact, I hardly expect he will want it again!"

"Not want it again?"

"No! Now Sir Horace *has* sent for him, I feel persuaded he will stay there; the Rector *quite* thinks so."

Lady Laura could hardly hide her chagrin. "I wanted him *so* to see Pauline, she is looking so pretty, all her good looks have come back, and who can say if they met! He is in such a different position *now!* Sir Horace may die any day, and then——?"

"Laura, I think you must put Gerald Lanyon out of *all* your calculations, matrimonial ones, certainly."

"And why! may I ask? replied her sister coldly"

"Because he is already engaged to be married."

"*What?*"

"Yes! He is engaged to a very charming woman."

"There, that will do! *Who* is it?" asked Lady Laura abruptly.

"Miss Higgins!"

"Miss Higgins! Then you knew it all

along. I must say, Louisa, it was hardly sisterly, you allowed me to come down under false pretences!" So then in her vexation Lady Laura divulged all her schemes, which the Rector's wife had perfectly seen through, long ago.

"Dear Laura! It was *your* wish, not mine, that you should come down to Langton, though I am always pleased to have you, and Pauline as well. But with regard to the cottage, it was quite optional your taking it."

"Well, we certainly shall not require it for more than three weeks," said her ladyship, ungraciously. "I expect Pauline will be bored to death as it is, as she cou'd not understand why I wanted to bury us both down here."

"Laura dear," said her sister affectionately, laying her kind gentle hand on her sister's shoulder. "Let Pauline be happy in her own way, don't scheme any more for her; you know she really loves young Vere. He is well off, true he is not titled, but what does that signify? I feel *sure* they will be happy. I think so much of Pauline's future character will depend upon her happiness. Nay, love," she added, with a smile, "I fancy she will settle the matter for herself, just as my pair of lovers have done."

"It does not seem right, or just," said Lady Laura, after she had digested the very unpleasant pill her sister had prepared for her, "that so much wealth should go together, it ought to be divided."

"I am *sure*, Laura, both Miss Higgins and Mr. Lanyon are the best people in the world to have wealth. They have such high and noble thoughts. It is quite delightful to hear them talk."

"So, *you* have been helping on these

affairs," said Lady Laura, sharply. "I daresay you think you are very clever."

"Oh, no, Laura," said her sister, colouring under the unpleasant scrutiny. "I am only so *glad* to think they are happy."

"I should have thought at your age you would have left off romance."

"Yes, dear! But not the pleasure of seeing others. happy."

Then the Rector came in, accompanied by Mr. Blythe, and nobody could be sulky in their presence. The Rector with his cheery, straight-to-the-point pleasant ways, and Percy Blythe, with his gay, good humour. So she gradually recovered her serenity, and began to reconcile herself to the inevitable marriage, which *she knew* would take place with (or without) her consent. And thus Gerald Lanyon was relegated to the limbo of forgotten things. He interested her no more.

14*

"Lady Louisa, when *does* Mrs. Grantley return?"

"Oh, not just yet, I believe. We ought not to complain, considering how much of her time and company she gives to us country people."

"No, indeed," replied Mr. Blythe, "only one misses her bright presence and pretty ways."

"She is a dear little woman," said the Rector.

I can't think whatever her brother does without her," said his wife.

"I hear he spends most of his time catching insects or beetles, or something unpleasant," said Lady Laura.

"My dear sister, allow me to tell you he has a *very* valuable collection of moths," corrected the Rector.

"Well, I hope he will keep them. I do not wonder his sister occasionally requiring to get out of such a stuffy atmosphere—camphor, and laudanum, and other poisons, isn't it?"

"I really can't say," said the Rector, laughing. "I do not collect or preserve such things myself, but I daresay it is a very interesting study."

"Very," said her ladyship, sarcastically, "going out at night, treacling the trees, and armed with a lantern and a net."

"I *think*, my dear, the treacling is done in the day, *ready* for the moths at night. But, as I observed before, I am not *sure* of anything."

"Mr. Blythe, I hope you will come and see us when we get settled at the cottage."

"I shall be only too pleased, Lady Laura. Can I help in any way?"

"Well, I should not be surprised! When you are off duty, you might come and see."

" Most certainly I will ! But as I am on duty *now* (there is the even-song bell), I will say good-bye."

And very soon the Rector went out for his last round, previous to dinner, but *the* ' Topic' was no more resumed between the sisters.

CHAPTER XIV

Miss Higgins did take a house in town, and she with Esmé and the household transferred themselves to Connaught Terrace, Hyde Park, and the two ladies thoroughly enjoyed it. Sir Ernest Beldon was their willing escort to all places of amusement. They even tempted the Rector and Lady Louisa to come up to them for a few days, and enjoy the pomps and vanities of this pleasant, if sinful, world. Of Gerald Lanyon, Hester had almost daily accounts, so that there was no drawback to her happiness. All her thoughts were concentrated upon the question of Esmé's. She saw day by day that Ernest Beldon was gaining ground but she used no persuasion to her child— she let things take their course.

"Esmé! would you not like to ride in the Park every now and then?"

"I should, Hester, but I don't think old Brownie would cut much of a figure in the Row."

"No, indeed!" said Hester, laughing heartily, as the fat, plethoric Brownie, comfortably turned out to grass at home, presented himself to her mind. "No! we must have a nice horse for you, dear. I will speak to Ernest Beldon about it. Men know all about these things so much better than women. He will be sure to look in this morning."

As they were yet speaking of him, he was announced.

"We were just talking about you, Ernest," said Hester.

"Indeed, Miss Higgins! It is pleasant hearing."

"Yes. I want Esmé to ride, as well as

drive, in the Park. But she must have a horse. Something very nice, for my little woman." And she looked affectionately at Esmé, as she stood gazing out of the window, and Ernest looked too, with eyes as much full of love as Hester's—too full, for Esmé turned her head, but not before Sir Ernest had seen a little tell-tale blush.

"I will look in at Tattersall's, they are sure to have something suitable there; you may depend upon it I will do my best."

"Don't stand out for price, Ernest, let it be as perfect as can be. I am going this morning to have her measured for her new habit."

"Well then, by the time the habit is ready, the steed will be likewise. By the bye, the Willises are in town, and are coming to call upon you. Shall you be a home this afternoon?"

"I will be, certainly! How is your sister, Ernest?"

"Much better for her German course of waters. It seems quite a fashionable complaint, this youthful rheumatism! Hortense is not eight-and-twenty. What business has she, and other young women of her age, with such an ancient complaint? I believe it is nothing in the world but that they want to have a nice little course of gambling at the tables, and a slight attack of these ailments is a convenient peg to hang a journey upon."

"Well, but, Sir Ernest, we have been there at different times without the rheumatism, and without the gambling," said Esmé from her place at the window.

"I only said, fair lady, that many young women *do* make it a pretence."

"Ah! they have husbands, no doubt," said she saucily, "and perhaps they would not take them otherwise. *Some* men like to go alone."

"They must be Goths then! I hate it! What commands for to-night, Miss Higgins?"

"Dinner at seven, 'Ours' at the Haymarket at eight-thirty.

"Do let us see it all, Hester! I am so anxious to see the Bancrofts in it! I would not miss a scrap!"

"That is why I have ordered dinner earlier, dear."

"Well, ladies, adieu! no, *au revoir* until seven o'clock. I shall go to Tattersall's now and let you know the result to-night. Get your habit all ready, Miss Esmé, or *I* should say under way."

She nodded her head, and he departed.

"Put your things on, dear," said Miss Higgins, "I have ordered the carriage for twelve, it is ten minutes to now."

Esmé left with her little pug "Prince," a gift of Sir Ernest, hugged in her arms. The door had hardly closed upon her, and Hester, for the second time that morning, was absorbed in a long letter from Gerald Lanyon. It was a letter that made her feel the years roll by, and that she was a young girl again, looking forward with the perfect conviction that life was a beautiful reality.

"Mr. Dashwood!" announced the footman. With a sigh Hester came back to earth. But being so very happy herself, she received him with more graciousness than was her wont.

"I did not know you were in town, Mr. Dashwood?"

"I had some business on hand, and that brought me up."

There was none of the usual stiff hauteur about Miss Higgins, on the contrary, there was a brightness, a graciousness which he thought (and hoped) must be in some way occasioned by himself. So he felt a fresh wave of confidence. He had been considered so irresistible, he was so undeniably handsome; his clothes the very perfection of perfect tailoring, and his figure faultless! And it would be almost impossible that he should not succeed with this cold and haughty personage, though to-day she looked almost good-looking! and certainly more *amiable* than *he* had ever seen her.

"Miss Higgins! I have come on an errand of deep interest" ("Esmé," thought Hester). "Can you not guess it?"

"I conclude I can, Mr. Dashwood. But I fancy, you will find—you are—too late!"

"Too, late! Dearest Miss Higgins! nay, let me say at once, dear Hester!

do not use these wretched words" (and he seized her hand tightly) "You have been my load-star my—"

"Are you referring to *me*, sir! by using this extraordinary language!" she cried, struggling angrily to release her hand.

"*You*, and you alone, Hester!"

"Then pray understand, most distinctly, that I consider your pretensions to my hand a positive insult!"

"An insult! Miss Higgins!" he exclaimed with rising colour. "If a man makes an honourable proposal to a woman, you must excuse me, if I fail to see the insult."

"Nevertheless, I maintain it is an insult! and a degrading one. For nearly two years have you, in season and out of season, been assiduously courting. Miss Curtis, working on the tender innocent heart of my young ward, until she loved you. And now you dare come to me, with your stereotyped arguments of love, forsooth. But let me just say, before the subject of Miss Curtis is dismissed, that I have every hope that she has, at last, found an object worthy of her generous heart."

"You are very much mistaken!" he answered, perfectly unaware that Esmé, who had just crossed the threshold, stood, holding back the heavy *portière*, in blank amazement, and at a sign from Hester, remained there.

"No, sir! I am not mistaken! And I must frankly add, I despise you *thoroughly!* And even had my hand been at my own disposal, which it is not, you can hardly imagine I should bestow it on one who, to my own knowledge, has long since given his heart to another woman!"

"But, believe me Miss Higgins, it was

only a man's passing fancy, a liking for a pretty child, for she is but a child still."

"Child or no child! The good, honourable man who seeks her for *herself* (and one has I believe already won her heart), will not receive her empty-handed, for on the day she marries *with my consent*, she receives, as her marriage *dot*, eight thousand pounds! And now, I must request you to retire. I have an immediate engagement." Then she rose to her full height, and pointed to the door.

Finding her face set against him, immovable, and severe as a sphinx, there was nothing left for him, but to pick up his soft felt hat, and turn to go—worsted in every way!—when to his horrified discomfiture, he saw Esmé standing in the doorway! pale, and scornful. The soft face that had always turned with such looks of love to him, was now stiffened into disdain. He rushed past her, his handsome face distorted with rage; he tore down the staircase, snatched his umbrella from the hall-porter, and hardly waited for that functionary to open the door. He flew into the street! "Fool! fool! that I have been! Pursuing the shadow, and losing the substance. And Esmé has eight thousand pounds!" Yes! there was the sting! The girl he *had* loved in his selfish way, was not after all, a penniless orphan! "It is that fiend of a woman!—that Quack's daughter, who is at the bottom of all this! And Esmé! Esmé! I have lost you, for you must have heard all!" And as the Rev. Cyril Dashwood flew along the road, his face· was not pleasant to behold.

* * * * *

"Esmé! Do you see that man in his true colours, at last? His mean sordid soul! Oh my dear! I do feel thankful that you had not bestowed yourself upon him. He would always have been hankering after *my* riches, if even he had married you."

"And yet, I think he did love me *once!*"

"Doubtless, you think so, but *the* person *he* loved, was the Reverend Cyril Dashwood."

"Yes, I fear so. Well!" said the girl with some sadness, "this interview which I unwillingly assisted at, has opened my eyes as to his character, and for the future I shall dismiss him from my thoughts. I feel sorry Hester! It is always hard to take down your gods from the pedestal, perhaps we put them up too high. Who knows?"

"Good gracious! Esmé, those poor horses have been standing *twenty minutes!*

Old Charles will look untold reproaches! I must fly, and put my bonnet on."

Miss Higgins' toilets were always rapid, and in a very few moments the two ladies were out, on business intent; and when they returned, an hour-and-a-half later, Esmé looked as bright and as bonnie as if no such things as lovers ever troubled her.

After lunch, Hester put her arm round Esmé. "Dearest, put on the pale blue velvet dress, with the chinchilla trimming, it suits you so well. I want you to look very nice this afternoon."

"Hester, you are always thinking how *I* look. I shall take you in hand, and see how you look."

"So you shall, dear."

"Well, what are you going to wear?"

"Oh, I don't know! Whatever Justine puts out."

"That is exactly what I expected."

15*

"Well, dear, ugly people should always dress quietly, and Justine generally puts me into black, you know, it is so safe."

"Safe, indeed! But you can't blame Justine. When she does try 'an elegant confection,' as she calls it, you hardly observe it; and put it on with the same indifference you do those ugly, black gowns you live in! Certainly! I must take you in hand, dear old Hester! You do want brightening up. Not your face, dear, that is sweet, but you *must* have some new gowns, which *I* shall see about."

"So you shall, dear! whenever you like." She would have promised anything, seeing the bright gay face, and manner of the young girl. She had been fearful, that that horrid interview in the morning, might have left lingering pain. But the fact was, Esmé's love for Cyril Dashwood

had died a natural death ; it had died hard
for want of nourishment, but it had died;
and his barefaced repudiation of *her* love
that morning, had given it the *coup de
grace*. And some one else, she would
hardly confess it, even to herself, had already
filled the vacant niche, and another god
reigned in his stead. She was going to
the theatre that night. She was to have a
new habit, and last, but not least, a
beautiful horse. Under all these circumstances, *could* any girl be sad ? Certainly
not! and she—she felt happy. So she
tripped up to her room to don the blue
velvet ; and by-and-by came down, looking so piquant, and so lovely, that Hester
was fain to take the little *mignon* face
between her hands, and kiss it fondly.

"I suppose now *I* must repair the
ravages of the day, and make *myself* pre-
sentable ? "

" That you must, dear ! "

" Sir Ernest Beldon ! "

" Miss Higgins, you must think I am a regular Jack-in-the-box, I am for ever turning up unexpectedly. But I have seen *such* a charming horse—suit you down to the ground, Miss Esmé."

" What colour is it ? " said Esmé, eagerly.

" Chesnut ! and it has a white star on its forehead."

" Has it a name ? "

" It has. The ' Duke,' at your service ! It will come round to-morrow, for you to see ; it has been ridden by a lady, and is very gentle, but I shall ride it myself first, and try it well."

" Thanks, dear Ernest, for your trouble," said Lester, well pleased. " Excuse me for a few moments, Esmé will take care of you ! "

"I wish you only would, Miss Esmé," said he, turning round as Miss Higgins closed the door behind her, and looking eagerly at the lovely face.

" Would what? "

" Take care of me ! "

"If there is anyone able to take care of themselves, it is Sir Ernest Beldon."

"Indeed not! I have very serious thoughts of going out to the Zulu war."

" To the wars? " said she, a trifle pale.

"Yes! You see if I am not wanted in England, I may be useful out there."

"But, who does not want you in England?"

"You, for one! "

"Oh, Sir Ernest! how *can* you say so? "

" Well, shall I stay? or go? "

" But it is not for me to decide."

" But it is! It is ' yes' or ' no '—only if I

stay you will have to take charge of me, or I shall be off, most certainly."

"But I can't decide all in a hurry like this!"

"Well! which side will the voting be? To go or to stay?"

"I suppose—you—must stay; but I shall not decide to-day!" she cried, and jumping away out of his reach, her face wreathed in saucy smiles. She knew her power only too well.

"You might put a fellow out of his misery!"

"No! I do not at all see the necessity for that; it is so good for you morally not to have everything your own way. I know when I was a small chit at school, this admirable precept was well drummed into my head."

"Well I do not mean to have it drummed into my heart, anyway! I have been wait-

ing over a year!—two years, I know!—that
is long enough in all conscience."

"Sir Ernest, excuse me, that is a
fiction!"

"It is a fact, Miss Esmé.   Will you promise without fail to make up your mind to-
night?"

"I will try, but really——"

"Sir Percy and Lady Willis!"

"Ernest!"

"Hortense!"

"Why, Ernest! we thought you were at
Heminglee."

"I was there, my dear sister, but a man
is not a fixture, like a tree!"

"Evidently! But where is Miss Higgins?
Oh, here she is!" as the door opened to
admit Hester.   "How well you are looking! and Miss Curtis, too; a vast improvement on what you were when I saw you at
Homberg last year! Do you remember?

Mr. and Mrs. Cohen and the Mountchesnys were there?"

"Yes, indeed! There have been changes since that. I hear the poor man is dead now, and died quite poor, comparatively speaking."

"Yes, that American house let him in for a lot."

"I suppose Mrs. Cohen is very badly off?"

"Oh no!" continued Sir Ernest, "by no means; she has a very comfortable little settlement."

"Ernest!" whispered his sister, "how did you know we should be calling here to-day?"

"Because, my dear! your letter announced that fact. It was forwarded to the club, and reached me this morning."

"Isn't there some attraction? Eh! Ernie?"

" *Peut-être.*"

" She will make a lovely Lady Beldon.
I will say that."

Her brother gave her an affectionate
little glance. She was his elder by three
years, and deeply attached to him.

" Is it quite settled ? "

" No ; but I hope soon to tell you that
it is."

" I expect you are glad to be home
again ? " said Hester to Sir Percy, who was
a great, hearty, good-natured man, who
infinitely preferred his turnips and his
stock to all the attractions of foreign travel.

" That I am ! It's my lady here who
likes all this racketing, not me. But I am
in time for the hunting—that's one comfort ! "

" I tell Percy he is getting too heavy, look
at the weight he will be ! I don't believe
he will have a horse fit to carry him."

" Oh yes, my lady! I have taken care of that, never fear ! "

" You know, Percy! I did my best to help you, if you only *would* have gone in for a good course of the waters ! "

" Beastly mess I was ! well ! why should I make myself ill ? I'm right enough," said he heartily. " And you know, Miss Higgins, my lady, in spite of the waters, and looking like a wax doll, can go across country like a bird."

" That she *can*," said her brother. I remember where she caught you up ! Eh, Willis ? and half pulled you out of the brook."

" That's true !" said Sir Percy, laughing heartily at the recollection. " That beast of mine pitched me clean overhead, into the dirtiest quagmire you ever saw, while my lady took it as neat as a new pin. By-the-by, I want a fresh mount for your sister. Have you seen anything likely to suit Hortense ? "

" I saw several this morning at Tattersall's. I am looking out for Miss Higgins, who is wanting one for Miss Curtis. Come round there by eleven to-morrow morning, there's a sale on, and we can look them over—earlier if you can, I am due here at twelve."

Very soon afterwards the friends separated.

And when Esmé was dressing for dinner, a bouquet arrived for her, composed of delicate roses, but in the centre was a sprig of white heather, the emblem of good luck. She knew then her fate was decided, so with a smile she put the heather in her dress! Hester saw it, but made no comment. She thought things had nearly reached their happy climax, so she would wait, it could not be for long.

" Dinner is served ! "

" Has Sir Ernest Beldon arrived, Lloyd ? "

" Yes, Ma'm. He is——"

" Here I am, Miss Higgins ! only a minute behind time !"

" We are punctual to a minute, you see."

He eagerly looked at Esmé, who rose from her seat by the fire. Was it the fire-light, or something else, that sent such a lovely colour over her face ? He saw the white heather. " Thank you my darling ! " he stooped and whispered low, and then gave his arm to Miss Higgins.

Lloyd was stolidly holding the door, apparently gazing into vacancy, waiting with decorous patience for his mistress' pleasure. Did he guess?—they always do find out everything. I think so.

The charming little dinner was over,

and the carriage at the door! Hester
fancied she had forgotten something! so
left Ernest and Esmé in the drawing-room,
he held the soft white wrap, and as he put
it round her, he kissed the soft face. "Ah,
Esmé, you are a little tyrant, you have
kept me waiting long enough, but you are
worth the waiting for."

"The fact is, I thought on the whole it
would not do to let you go off to the
wars. So if you still think of going, I had
better accompany you!"

"Then I must stay at home, if only to
look after you. Do give me one kiss,
Esmé, before we start!"

"Just one, then!" and she stood on tip-
toe, and daintily raised herself to his
height. He held her prisoner.

"Do you really love me, Esmé?"

"Really! Ernest. Yes! But you are
annihilating my dress! I shall look like

an old rag bag. Now, sir ! If you will let
me go, I will give you one of my lovely
roses ! "

" I would quite as soon have these close
at hand," said he, touching her cheek, and
giving her one more embrace, let her
go. " Now for the white rose, and then
put it in my coat, Esmé. Here is Miss
Higgins ! "

"Here is one for you Hester ! darling,"
and she pinned one in her friend's dress,
and kissed her with unwonted affection.
And then Hester knew it was accomplished.

" Let me speak to you, Ernest, before
you go to-night, after our return from the
play."

·· " I intended to ask your ' Highness ' for
an audience ! " said he to Hester as they
descended the stairs. " I have much to
tell you ! "

"I am so glad, dear friend! for you and for her!"

"You are the truest friend a man could ever have," he answered, much moved.

It was late when they came from the play. They went into the dining-room, where a cheerful fire awaited them, as well as some substantial refreshment.

"Now, Miss Esmé, you will be pleased to remember your gay wings will very shortly be clipped. My home wants a mistress. I will give you two months, not a moment more."

"But really, dear Ernest, I could not leave my dear Hester in that hurry! Indeed, I could not."

"What is that about, Hester?" said that lady returning to the room.

"Why it is just this, Miss Higgins. This small personage, after promising to be my wife, declines to be married, and does not in the least care how badly I fare at home."

"Oh! How can you say such things?" said Esmé, colouring up prettily. "He *insisted* upon my having him, Hester—indeed he did, and yet, how can I leave you, darling?"

"Esmé, dearest, you have made me perfectly happy. I do think we women want a staff to lean on. (I believe I have made that observation before," she said, with a merry little aside to Esmé), "and I like your staff dear." She held out her hand to Ernest, who warmly grasped it with both his, and with her other arm she encircled Esmé.

"You will cherish my dear child?"

"That I will," he replied, with affectionate earnestness.

And who could doubt it ? as they looked on the kind, honest face, so frank and open, so true and kind.

" And now, if you please, Miss Esmé, you will be so good as to take your supper, and then retire to bed, not because you have been naughty, but because you have been good. I want to talk over a little business with Ernest. You won't be jealous, eh, darling ? " said Miss Higgins, laughingly.

" Oh, Hester ! you are a teaze ! " So after the supper things had been removed, and the dignified Lloyd had placed the candles outside the dining-room door, in readiness for their respective owners, and finally disappeared for the night, Ernest lighted Esmé's candle, and gave her a very hearty kiss.

" Remember, sweetheart, ' The Duke' will be round at twelve for your inspection, to-morrow."

16*

The bright young face nodded gaily, and when she reached the first landing, she detached the flowers from her bodice, and pelted him gaily. He carefully collected all the scattered blossoms, and placed them reverently in the breast pocket of his coat.

"Oh, love! young love! bound in thy rosy band,
    Let sage or cynic prattle as he will,
    These hours, and only these, redeem life's years
        of ill!"

"The Duke" made his appearance at twelve, accompanied by his attendant, Sir Ernest Beldon, and Sir Percy Willis. He was trotted up and down for the inspection of his future mistress, and both ladies pronounced him simply charming, which, indeed, was only his fair due. His glossy skin shone like satin, his dainty limbs, nervous, yet strong, while his beautiful head and soft dark eyes completed his victory.

"That's about as pretty a bit of horse-flesh as I've seen this many a long day," said Sir Percy, who had come up-stairs to the ladies. "I have found something for Hortense, but my lady's won't come up to that, it isn't the same long price, though, for one thing, not that it's a bad mount— but Beldon wants to know what you think of ' The Duke ' ladies."

"Oh, he is lovely! Sir Percy," said Esmé, almost trembling with eagerness. "Do ask Sir Ernest when I can ride him."

"To-morrow, young lady," said the young man, in person, running up the stairs, to hear what his betrothed had to say. "How do you like my taste, or rather choice ? "

"Oh, Ernest ! he is simply a darling ! I long to kiss him."

"Kiss me instead! I can kiss him, after-wards, it will be all the same ! "

"Pardon me! It will be *quite* different. I want to make love to him on my own account, so that he will love me, do you see?"

"Well you might just make acquaintance on the doorstep. They tell me, he loves little golden pippins, but is particular about the right sort!"

"I *believe* we have some left from dessert!" And down she ran to find out.

"Excuse me, Miss Higgins!" said Sir Ernest, as he too disappeared.

Both Sir Percy and Miss Higgins laughed.

"Ernest informs me he is coming round to our hotel, this afternoon, to tell us some news! It strikes me, I can guess it!" And Sir Percy chuckled at his own discernment.

"I expect you can. As we are on the subject, I wish you to be one of Esmé's trustees. I told Ernest I should settle eight thousand pounds as her marriage portion."

" You are most generous, Miss Higgins!"

" Her love, has been beyond price. You cannot understand how lonely a woman may be, even with wealth."

"Well, no. Wealth always seems to me one of the nicest acquaintances you can well have. Perhaps, because I have not seen too much of him."

"Here come our 'children,'" said he as the two young people—breathless, but happy—came into the room."

" Oh, Hester! He did enjoy the apples. And I did kiss his soft nose! Charles quite appreciates him. He says, he won't be ashamed to take me out in the park now."

" He will not very often have that privilege!" said Sir Ernest, stiffly.

"Charles is a dear old thing! only grumpy," said Esmé.

"Well, Ernest! are you going back to lunch with your sister? or what are your arrangements?"

"I will go with you. I have told the man to take 'The Duke' round to your stables, Miss Higgins. Old Charles, your amiable functionary, has condescended to see to his comfort."

"Thank you, Ernest," said Miss Higgins, with a smile. "We will go round this afternoon, and hurry the tailor about Esmé's habit. And, Sir Percy! will you bring your wife round to lunch with me to-morrow? but I want you very early, because the two impatient young people will wish to be off for their ride! And I— well I want to see them set off, and we might drive for an hour, if that will be agreeable."

"If my lady has not made any other engagement, 1 shall be *very* pleased to bring her."

"*1* shall make her break them, if she has," said the young baronet gaily.

He spoke with the airy confidence of one who generally has his own way with women folk, especially his own.

"We shall be round, never fear, at twelve o'clock. *A bientôt chérie.*"

"Good-bye, Ernest, dear."

"I *can't* think which of my pets I shall love the best, the 'Prince,' or the 'Duke'!" said she, mischievously ignoring his farewell.

"As long as you keep a large supply for me, you can do as you like about them. I shall not be jealous."

"Oh, Hester! what a dear darling you are. I am so happy ! My very own mother could not have been more tender or generous.

"Then, I am repaid. Nay, love! we have both cause for deep gratitude. Our lines have been cast in pleasant places."

"Now dear, we must really ' to business,' there will be all your trousseau to see about; we must have Justine into the conclave, she knows so much. And after we have been about your habit, we might begin this afternoon ! "

And, there we will leave them for the present, deeply intent on the business in hand.

"I cannot help feeling, Ernest, the more one sees of Miss Higgins the more one realises her heart is of gold. She is a noble woman," said his sister, as they sat chatting after lunch. "I am so glad, dear boy ! you will be happy. Your Esmé is the sweetest, prettiest little creature I

have ever seen! and having lived in the
atmosphere of goodness and honour nearly
all her life, she will be free from the hateful
blemishes of the 'society girls,' with their
slang, their forwardness, their 'awfully nice,
don't you know.' They are all made on one
pattern, if there is anything to say in their
favour. They are just a peg higher than
the 'Mashers,' for they do say what they
think, and those inane youths of the period
generally *can't* think, and consequently
have nothing to say."

"Upon my word, Hortense, you seem
to be qualifying yourself to sit in the seat
of the scornful, and no mistake! What say
you, Percy? Laying down the law, eh?"

"Oh," said Sir Percy, puffing out little
wreaths of smoke from his cigar, "I
always give my lady her head. There's
nothing like it; after she has let off the
steam, she is as mild as a moonbeam!"

"Don't talk such nonsense, Percy! I have heard you say the same thing yourself!"

"Then don't quote me, my dear, let it be all original matter, when you do hold forth."

"I think it is this," said Sir Ernest, thoughtfully, "These young fellows are nearly all young—not cut their wisdom teeth! But, I feel sure, if these same boys were left to rough it, say out in the wilds, or in the thick of war, all these borrowed airs and graces would drop off them like a ragged raiment! and we should have the genuine article—the pluck, the endurance, the making-the-best-of all difficulties, such as English fellows always show—the pride and glory of their country! She has turned them out by hundreds! thousands!"

"Hear, hear!" said Sir Percy, "that's

it! that's what we expect of *our* boy, eh, Hortense? when he grows up; poor little chap, he is learning it by doses at the county Grammar School."

"Dear child! he is just ten now, and so sweet!" said his mother.

"Mind he gets out for my wedding, Hortense! I should not think it a *fait accompli* without Phil."

"He shall come, dear!" said Lady Willis brightly. "When is the wedding to be?"

"Oh, about February."

"Losing no time, young man!"

"Certainly not! Now you and Hortense have forsaken Heminglee—it is *horrible!* and I am not so fond of my own company as some people. Hortense, do be in time to-morrow at Connaught Terrace, I know Miss Higgins wants to show off Esmé on 'The Duke.'"

" How much did you give for him? " asked Sir Percy.

" Oh, never mind! it is a present I mean to make her."

" We will come, dear! " said his sister affectionately.

" Thanks, Hortense. By-the-bye, when you write to Phil, give him this tip from uncle Ernest," and he put a sovereign into her hand.

" *Thank* you, Ernest, for thinking of Phil. He will be pleased! "

" I should *rather* think so! When I was a boy half-a-crown was considered a very handsome *douceur*. Boys and girls are all spoilt now-a-days," said Sir Percy.

" Never mind! they will take it out in the next generation! and if we only live we shall see our grandchildren marvels of propriety! "

" I think very proper children are

deceitful," said Lady Willis, in answer to her brother.

"Ha! ha!" laughed Sir Percy. "*Our* boy is rascal enough, I can answer for that. He certainly is not proper."

END OF VOLUME I.

PRINTED BY
KELLY AND CO., GATE STREET, LINCOLN'S INN FIELDS,
AND KINGSTON-ON-THAMES.

www.ingramcontent.com/pod-product-compliance
Lightning Source LLC
Chambersburg PA
CBHW031345020726
47499CB00005B/1411